BELIEF

BELIEF

The second book in the Marcus Kline trilogy

CHRIS PARKER

urbanepublications.com

First published in Great Britain in 2017 by Urbane Publications Ltd
Suite 3, Brown Europe House, 33/34 Gleaming Wood Drive, Chatham, Kent
ME5 8RZ
Copyright © Chris Parker, 2017

A CIP catalogue record for this book is available from the British Library.

ISBN 978-1-909273-23-8
MOBI 978-1-909273-25-2
EPUB 978-1-909273-24-5

Design and Typeset by Julie Martin
Cover by Chandler Design Co.

Printed and bound by CPI Group (UK) Ltd, Croydon, CR0 4YY

urbanepublications.com

The publisher supports the Forest Stewardship Council® (FSC®), the leading international forest-certification organisation.
This book is made from acid-free paper from an FSC®-certified provider. FSC is the only
forest-certification scheme supported by the leading environmental organisations, including Greenpeace.

This one's for Vic.

Belief: *noun*
An acceptance that something exists or is true,
especially one without proof.

Alice laughed. 'There's no use trying,' she said.
'One can't believe impossible things.'
'I daresay you haven't had much practice,' said the Queen.
'When I was your age, I always did it for half-an-hour a day.
Why, sometimes I've believed as many as six impossible
things before breakfast.'

Lewis Carroll

'The solidity of the edge is next to the emptiness of the fall.'

Epiah Khan

PART 1

DOUBT

1

There are two kinds of dream.

We experience both kinds.

The first is the kind that reflects something that has already happened. It occurs whenever the subconscious takes a memory and re-presents it in its own peculiar fashion, adding twists and turns and changes.

This kind of dream prompts the question, '*What do you think that means?*' There are libraries and shops filled with books promising to explain the symbolism these dreams are supposed to contain.

The second kind of dream provides the seed for future growth. It occurs when we are seeking an answer to a question or a solution. It throws up the Eureka moment, the flash of insight that provides the unexpected and unbelievably brilliant resolution.

This is the kind of dream that prompts the question, '*Where the hell did that come from?*' Only it didn't come from any kind of hell at all. Oh, no. It came from the very opposite place. From the almighty subconscious, daring us to believe that we have more power than we can possibly imagine.

Both kinds of dream have one thing in common. They are both influenced by our beliefs. They are influenced by our beliefs about our own personal strengths and weaknesses, about our relationships, our society, and our planet. They are influenced by our beliefs about the power of the past, the possibilities in the present and the nature of the future.

Ultimately they are influenced by our beliefs about the meaning of it all.

Our dreams, then, are no different from our waking lives.

Both are shaped, delivered and evaluated by our beliefs. We create and then view our world through the prism of our beliefs. We all do this. Everyone of us. Every moment of every day.

That's how powerful beliefs are. More powerful than anything else human beings create. More powerful even than the most powerful nuclear weapon. Actually, beliefs are the invisible trigger we use to justify firing such weapons. More than that, they are the trigger we fire every time we set out to cause *any* form of deliberate harm.

Beliefs. The biggest, the best and, sometimes, the baddest of everything there is.

Of course, as you read that you are forced to come to one of three conclusions.

One, that you don't believe me.

Two, that you do believe me.

Three, that you are undecided.

I should warn you that if you chose the third option you will, as you read what follows, be forced to get off the fence and settle for one of the other two.

Actually, to be honest with you, you will be forced to choose option number two. You will have to agree with me. You will come to realise that beliefs rule. You will find yourself smiling, somewhat ironically perhaps, at the delicious paradox that states:

The beliefs we create, create the world we believe in. And that's a fact.

And it is.

Pure and simple.

For better or for worse.

2

Marcus Kline stared at his computer screen as he sat in the almost complete darkness of his study and read the words again.

For better or for worse.

One hour ago he had begun writing his new book, *Belief*. Now the first few hundred words were written.

Marcus stared at the computer screen and wondered if the opening page or so was too abrupt. Too challenging. Too personal, perhaps?

For better or for worse.

When he and Anne-Marie had married ten years ago today – it was now twenty minutes passed midnight – they had designed their own, unique ceremony. It had been non-religious in nature obviously; a very personal sharing of emotions and commitment, with readings and music and promises from a range of sources, some created by Marcus himself.

They had divided the ceremony into two distinct parts. The one they shared with others and the one they shared only with each other. It was during this secret, intimate act, performed late at night on a private beach on the East Coast of Malaysia, with a full moon casting its light onto the South China Sea they shared the only vow that could be found in the Christian marriage service.

For better or for worse.

Marcus eased back in his chair, the computer screen temporarily forgotten, his eyes closing as he relived the experience. It took only a moment for the memory to spark the question *Just who am I writing this book for?*

Marcus's eyes opened automatically. His heartbeat quickened.

When Anne-Marie had told him, twenty-four hours after the killer Ethan Hall had been shot and captured, that she had life-threatening ovarian cancer, that she needed him to use his skills to help her combat the illness, Marcus had been almost overcome with fear.

It was a fear laced with guilt and self-recrimination, combining fear of loss with fear of failure, fear that he wasn't the person he believed himself to be with the fear that he was.

I know who I am, he thought. *I'm a supremely talented, selfish bastard who has built a global reputation as the world's greatest Communicator and Influencer whilst forgetting that I promised for better or for worse.*

The fear Marcus had felt when Anne-Marie first told him of her illness, the fear he still felt, was the nearest thing to a perfect fear he could dare to imagine. Made perfect by the fact that, when Anne-Marie broke the news and made her plea, he had been on the brink of telling her that he wanted a divorce.

Only he hadn't. Not given her illness and her need for help. Not when the unbelievable stress of being targeted by Ethan Hall had made him begin to consider and question so many things about himself and his relationships. Not when things were clearly so, so, bad.

And now, six months later, here he was.

Here *they* were.

Living in rented accommodation for the first time since their student days. They had found it impossible to stay in their much-loved detached house in the Park in the centre of Nottingham city. Ethan Hall had come within minutes of killing Marcus in that very house and his presence had infested every room. It was a presence they could not shift.

So they had moved out and rented. Moved to the outskirts of the village of Woodborough. Anne-Marie had wanted to be able to look out of the windows and see fields and nature and space. Marcus was only ever going to go along with her wishes. He knew that environment was a powerful influencing force and he needed every ally he could get to help him save his wife.

He had, he acknowledged, played his part in making things worse between them. The illness had then taken it to a whole new level. Now he was going to prove to Anne-Marie that there was nothing so bad that they couldn't beat it together.

He owed her that.

He needed it for himself.

He was a selfish bastard.

And the world was changing. He couldn't help but feel it was for the worse. He couldn't help but think that in the future his skills would be needed more than ever. He had to change to meet it. He had to save his wife first. If he couldn't do these things, he really wasn't sure he would be able to live with himself.

Marcus Kline nodded in acknowledgement of his self-evaluation. As he did so his mind instinctively went in search of something more positive. It didn't have time.

His silent introspection was cut short abruptly when his wife began screaming.

3

It was a dream.

The first kind.

The sort in which a past event is re-presented as a nightmare.

Anne-Marie's nightmare, playing like an unwanted photo essay, was a collection of images showing – reliving – all the medical procedures she had been forced to endure.

In the dream they flashed through her mind with ever-increasing speed. The drips and the drugs. The tubes and the tests. The catheters and the cuts. The x-rays and the monitoring. The scans, the stockings and the sampling. The pain and the painkillers. The biopsies and the blood.

The great reveal.

The great removal.

Ovaries and womb. Omentum and tumour – as much of that as they could cut out.

They called it interval debulking surgery.

She felt her womanhood had been ripped away, sacrificed in the hope she might live a longer life. In the belief she could find a new sense of identity.

The dream forced Anne-Marie awake, crying and screaming, as it always did.

Marcus was there within seconds. 'It's going to get better. I promise.' He lay on the bed, his arms encircling her.

Anne-Marie felt his breath on her face as he spoke. She could hear the confidence and control in his voice. She could feel the strong beat of his heart, faster than normal but reassuring nonetheless. She pressed against his chest. His left hand moved into the small of her back as she fought to control her breathing, to get the images from her mind.

'I don't know who I am anymore,' she managed eventually. 'I can't get back...I can't get back what I've lost, who I was. I don't know how to fight this.'

Anne-Marie felt Marcus's silent inhalation.

'It's only natural,' he said gently, his left hand beginning to move in a tight, clockwise motion, applying gentle pressure to the base of her spine. 'The key is to be accepting of how you are right now, and to believe that your sense of who you are will resurface more positively than ever before. It's still there, inside. You are here. Can you feel it?'

'Yes.' The word escaped before Anne-Marie even had chance to decide what question she was answering.

'You have to avoid viewing your own body as an opponent,' Marcus said, his voice softening into little more than a whisper. 'Truly. You have to avoid going to war with yourself, because war creates collateral damage and if your own mind and body are the battlegrounds, then the collateral damage has to occur there. You know this. We keep talking about it.'

'It's just too easy to think that I'm fighting for my life.'

'When the truth is, you're living through a new experience. An experience that's asking you to focus on the here and now, to breathe in the moment, to dissolve the artificial structures of past and future. An experience that's urging you to be gentle with yourself, to realise, remember and engage with the fact that most of your body is healthy and well. Go into this deeply, with curiosity, respect and care, just as when taking a photo of a new subject.'

'I know how to do that.'

'Of course. It's an important part of who you are. A very special part. Only you can share your experience in such a special way. Remember that. Only you, right?'

'Yes. Only me.'

That morning Anne-Marie had walked out into the fields, into the gently sloping valley surrounding the house, and taken a series of photos of the horizon. She wanted a new and meaningful addition to the very special photo essay titled *Far from the Shore: The Life and Death of an Ovarian Cancer* she was creating and sharing through her Facebook page. She was supporting this with a carefully edited diary and a selection of thoughts posted via her Blog and Twitter account.

In the months since Anne-Marie had started posting, she had attracted significant attention and support. It helped, of course, that as an internationally famous photographer she had many friends in the media and the arts who reported and promoted both her story and her work.

None of them, though, could possibly do for her the things her husband could. None of them could help find her new self, the one capable of recovery. She was, she thought, blessed to be married to a man like him. This man. Her man. She just prayed he was here because of love rather than obligation.

'Go back to sleep,' Marcus whispered. 'I'll keep the dream away.'

Anne-Marie closed her eyes and pressed even closer against him. She tried not to think of their future. She concentrated instead on her breathing and his closeness and the smell of his skin and the feel of the bed.

I need to believe, she reminded herself.

4

In a coma there is no space for either beliefs or dreams.

That was Ethan Hall's experience.

He had been in what the medical staff had called a coma for nearly six months. For him it had just been an altered state of consciousness. Throughout that time he had been able to hear everything people said about him. He could feel whenever they touched him. With his eyes closed, he could even feel them staring at him.

More incredible still, he had known when he was awake and when he was asleep. Before the experience, it had never occurred to him that people who were comatose could actually fall asleep. But now he knew it to be so.

Only, during his coma-sleep he felt he was entering a different world. If the coma had taken him away from the waking state, sleeping within his coma took him one significant step further. It created another layer of separation. Ethan welcomed it. He was used to being remote, to being distant and different from those around him.

He had realised many years ago that he experienced the everyday world of nature, society and people far more fully and richly than anyone else alive. He had become accustomed to the fact that he could see and hear the realities of life in ways no one else could. He knew he was unique and that he possessed a unique understanding and insight into everything and everyone he had ever encountered. Because of that he feared nothing. Because of that he sank willingly into the special depths of his coma-sleep.

The visions were waiting for him. They were not dreams. They were far more pure than any dream could ever be. They were the future. His future. Shown with clarity and precision and certainty.

Ethan Hall did not believe in fate. He did not accept that the course of a person's life was mapped out with unavoidable inevitability. If that was the nature of life it meant some people had been born only so that he could kill them. And, significant as he was, he couldn't bring himself to consider that possibility with any degree of seriousness.

No, his victims died because he chose them and then made it happen. That's how life worked. You made a decision and then you did whatever was necessary to turn it into reality. That was one of the few things he and Marcus Kline would have agreed upon.

Ethan knew that the visions he encountered in his coma-sleep were not the detailed foretellings of a well-laid cosmic plan, but rather the workings of his own subconscious showing him just what he was capable of achieving and how precisely to go about it.

So he felt secure and safe within his coma and, because the visions showed him what lay ahead, it never once crossed his mind he would stay in that state forever. In many ways, the coma was the most pure experience he had ever known. It did not require any form of consideration or interpretation. It provided freedom from the need for analysis or belief. It was simply *was*.

Ethan Hall found himself expanding and growing in its timelessness.

Then his eyes opened.

The world looked even brighter than he remembered it. His senses were sharper than they had ever been. He was, he realised, at the start of a new life. And he was beginning it with a level of sensory acuity even he found amazing.

I have been reborn.

Ethan particularly enjoyed it when, only a few hours after he had started talking, the policeman responsible for his arrest, Detective Chief Inspector Peter Jones, visited him.

Jones's motive was as obvious to Ethan as the predatory instinct he naively believed he kept hidden. Ethan lay very still and watched and listened as the policeman explained why he had been arrested and then read him his rights. Occasionally Ethan closed his eyes. He could actually smell the hunter's instinct gushing from the physically unassuming man sitting next to his bed. And that was a weakness.

It will prove to be fatal, Ethan promised himself as his mind went back in a calm, disassociated way to the instant when he had been shot. Two police bullets in the chest.

Tap. Tap.

Fired literally seconds before he had started scalping Marcus Kline. Two bullets tracing their distinct colours through the air. Bullets he could actually see spiralling towards him, bullets he would have avoided if the explosion of colour emanating from the officer who pulled the trigger had not distracted him. He was a man who, despite his ability with a firearm, was clearly a very different animal to the one sitting by his bedside.

'I'll leave you now,' Peter Jones said shifting fractionally in his chair.

Ethan could see that he secretly wanted to stay and ask more questions. He contained his smile as easily as he contained his visions. Timing, he knew, was everything. Especially when planning a revelation.

'I'd rather you stayed.' Ethan said it straight-faced. It was perhaps the most obvious *fuck-me* line of all time, only believable if you delivered it as if you didn't know that. Or didn't care.

Peter Jones did his best to hide his surprise. It would have worked with a blind man. Ethan felt his power coursing through his veins. He said, 'I'd like to talk, but only to you. Not to a surgeon or a nurse or any of those people. Do you understand? We've shared something special together. I nearly died. It has changed me. Do you understand?'

The detective nodded. 'I'm happy to let you talk, Ethan. I need to remind you though that you are under caution and I will make notes and anything you say can be used in evidence. Do you understand that?'

It was Ethan's turn to nod. 'Of course.' And then, 'Tell me, why are there two police officers outside my room and not just one?'

Peter Jones didn't blink. His face barely twitched. His heartbeat didn't alter. All in all he did an excellent job of receiving the question. Ethan saw how quickly he worked out what must have happened.

'You're right, a nurse told me,' he said. 'I'm only asking you about it because I thought in situations like this it was customary to post only one officer.'

Jones answered immediately. He didn't attempt to lie. 'Customary, yes. Compulsory, no. As with everything else we do, we deploy our manpower according to need. For all sorts of reasons, I thought it necessary to have a couple of officers outside your room at all times.'

'Should I take that to mean you regard me as a special risk?'

'I certainly think you are special.' Jones maintained eye contact as he spoke.

Ethan enjoyed the compliment and the honesty. It made sense, though. No one could lie to him successfully. He could see too much. He could hear too clearly.

'You are right, Ethan murmured, 'I am special.'

'Do you still feel that? Even now?' The detective did his best to keep a sense of victory out of his voice.

'You mean, do I still feel special even though you were able to arrest me? Of course I do. Firstly, you need to remember that sometimes being arrested is a sign of greatness. They arrested Gandhi. And Luther King. And Mandela. All innocent of everything apart from the fact they were life changing and different. And I am equally innocent. Until, or unless, you can prove otherwise.

'Secondly, you didn't beat me. We both know that. The arrest was a result of your good fortune. It was a matter of luck, not skill. You do acknowledge that, don't you?'

Peter Jones was silent for a moment. It was clear to Ethan that the notion of luck resonated uncomfortably within him. He regrouped and said, 'The very final part of it, yes, that was the result of an unexpected opportunity. As for the rest, we were closing in on you.'

'You were not closing in on me, detective. You were closing in on an unknown killer. A killer who remains unknown and free. A killer you are obliged to ignore until I am found innocent.'

'You won't be found innocent because you are not. So, whatever you might think, or hope, or believe, you will never get a chance to kill again.'

'You seem to be deliberately ignoring the fact that I haven't killed anyone, ever. It's because I am different – better – than the rest of you, better even than Marcus Kline, that you have decided I am a killer. That I'm evil. A monster, even. It's because you need to put your failings behind you that you are so keen to gain a conviction, regardless of the truth.'

'It's interesting to hear you practicing your story so soon. You've haven't been conscious for long and already you are preparing your defence.'

'I'm not preparing anything. I don't need to. And I certainly don't need to now. More importantly, you should know that your assumption is ill founded. To say I have only been conscious briefly implies I was unconscious before that. Nothing could be further from the truth.'

'Are you suggesting you were faking the bullet wounds and the coma?

'The wounds are real. We both know that. I suspect, though, that the man who shot me continues to see them more clearly and painfully than I do. I suspect they wake him at night.'

'He's doing fine.' The words were out before Peter could stop them.

The synesthete saw the colour of the lie and licked his lips, slowly and deliberately. 'It's quite an interesting paradox, isn't it?' he said. 'When the man who was shot recovers more quickly than the man who pulled the trigger?'

The detective didn't answer.

'Still, 'Ethan went on, 'such is life. And, just to be really clear, the coma was a most wonderful experience. Given that, would you please be so kind as to pass on a message to Marcus for me? Would you do that?'

Ethan didn't wait for a reply. It was time for the revelation. 'Please tell him the coma was a room in the schoolhouse I had never visited before. It was a place where I learnt so much. Please tell him I am brighter than ever.'

Peter Jones stood up. This time he made no attempt to keep the emotion, the anger, from his face. 'I'm a policeman not a postman,' he said. 'And no one, including Marcus, cares what you believe happened to you whilst you were laying here unconscious, being kept alive by the skill of the medical staff. This conversation is over.'

He turned his back to the bed and the smiling prisoner it contained and left the room without glancing back.

5

Marcus Kline couldn't turn his back on anything right now. Truth be told, his back felt like it was being crushed by the burden he was carrying.

The weight of his responsibility, his commitment, to Anne-Marie was increased by his defeat to the words, will and influence of Ethan Hall and by the fact that he really didn't like himself anymore.

I am burdened but not defeated.

That was the best he could tell himself, that and the constant repetition of his belief that a person grew stronger by carrying an ever-greater weight.

Only as the weight increased so did the doubt in his ability to save Anne-Marie from her cancer. It kept him awake during the darkness of the night. It made sleep almost impossible.

So he had decided to use that time productively. He had planned a new book and started writing. About belief, of all things. About the very topic at the heart of his current crisis. And you couldn't write about belief without also addressing doubt.

Marcus knew the source of his doubt. It was Ethan Hall. The man who had proven he was not the greatest influencer on the planet. Now, when he needed to be at his confident, most arrogant best he was plagued with doubt for the first time in his life. The fact that he had several decades of success behind him, that he had advocates and clients and admirers and fans at every level of society and in most countries on the planet counted for nothing. Ethan Hall was king. There was no escaping it.

Marcus looked at his watch: 2.20am. He had held Anne-

Marie for more than thirty minutes, long after she had fallen asleep again, and then returned to his computer. Only the words he hoped to write had disappeared behind the doubt and the dislike.

Both made worse by the fact that Ethan Hall had come out of his coma. Marcus knew, although Peter Jones had been careful not to say, that the Detective Chief Inspector doubted his ability to contain the synesthete.

The thought of a free Ethan Hall terrified Marcus. He had lost to the man once and he hadn't improved his skill since then. The truth – the truth that kept repeating inside him – was that he was lucky to have survived. He was here now because of a fluke. And if Ethan came after him again, what were the chances of being lucky for a second time?

Answer: Very limited at best.

Why couldn't he make himself believe that he could win?

Answer: Because he was damaged goods.

That was the bottom line. However good he had been, he had lost some of that edge, that essential self-belief, during his encounter with Ethan.

Belief and Doubt. Two sides of the most valuable coin. So close. So connected. So far apart.

Marcus Kline looked out of the window. The fields around him were invisible in the pure darkness of the country night. Whenever he had looked out from their old home, he had always seen lights in other houses, the occasional lights from a car; there had always been clear signs of life. Here, at night, there was nothing. Nothing outward. And that left only one place to go.

Inward.

That used to be his most private and powerful home. It used to be. Before doubt. Before the other side of the coin. Before Ethan Hall.

Marcus couldn't go there now; he certainly couldn't stay there. Homes are ruined when a killer visits them. That was what Peter Jones had told him. Every type of home, no exceptions, even the home you carry inside yourself.

Marcus sat, unmoving, staring into the darkness that surrounded the rented house. It was impenetrable.

6

Ethan Hall was also awake in the middle of the same night. For him the ceiling in his room didn't exist. There were no limits. And now there was only one policeman standing guard on his hospital door.

Only one.

Just one normal human being who happened to be a policeman. A man who no doubt craved repetition in his life just like the rest of the herd – that dull, grey, unthinking mass known by everyone else as society.

Ethan had learnt long ago that the herd created and then depended upon repetition. It was the safety net used by those who never actually travelled high in the first place. More importantly, it was the ultimate example of how a safety net becomes a comfort blanket before morphing slowly and gently into a see-through plastic bag clinging onto your head, pulling tighter and tighter with every breath, seeping into every crevice of your face, leaving no room for anything other than death.

Only the herd didn't realise it was dead. Dead as a collective and as individuals. Their senses, their most basic, natural and essential connection with the rest of the world, were all-but non-existent. The herd was, in the most disgusting meaning of the word, *senseless*. Dead to everything but their own, personal, limited, black-and-white perspectives.

Ethan Hall's perspective was anything but black and white. To him every aspect of the world was filled with colour and energy. He could see the colour of every emotion and every word. Fear and doubt, hope and belief were as visible to Ethan as paintings hanging on a wall. It had been that way since childhood.

When the doctors first identified his synaesthesia, they told his father it was a rare neurological condition that made an individual's senses hugely responsive to stimulation. They said it could be managed with help. Even as a young boy Ethan had known to ignore them. He had known – had seen – that they just wanted to emphasise their so-called expertise and authority. He had known his synaesthesia was a gift, a starting point. He had been proven right. As he actively worked to develop his abilities the world became a multi-sensory art gallery of opportunity. And power.

The need for repetition didn't apply to him. He was not a replica. Nor could he be copied. He was free.

Free to leave the hospital whenever he wanted. They couldn't hold him no matter what they tried. They didn't know that. But he did. His stay was almost over. He had people to see. Things to do. Changes to make.

Ethan Hall softened himself into the bed and looked up at the ceiling through eyes that were only half-open. He could see the night sky. He could see what no one else could. His future was about to begin.

7

Anne-Marie woke to find her husband lying beside her, watching her. His right arm reached out and she instinctively moved to him, resting her head on his shoulder. His arm curled around her, his hand stroking her upper arm.

He had already opened the bedroom curtains. She could see the early morning sun and the fresh, bright June sky offering their invaluable encouragement to the fields and trees that surrounded the house. She breathed in deeply trying to draw it all in, to breathe in the sky through the aroma of Marcus.

He smiled as if he knew what she was doing.

'It's a fine morning,' he said. 'Clear and fresh.'

'It's always been my favourite time of year.'

'I know.'

'And Autumn is yours.'

'It used to be. I'm not so sure these days.'

'What's changed?'

'Having this view.' Marcus eased himself into an upright position. Anne-Marie followed suit. They were quiet for a moment, just looking.

'Nature teaches us everything we need to know about change,' Marcus mused. 'If we look and listen and feel, She's offering it all to us. And we're a part of nature, perhaps the most important part.

'Behind our unnecessary internal chatter we all know how to move things on. Deep inside we all know how to create and manage change, how to turn thoughts into the best of words and words into the best of actions. We all do that in so many ways. Right?'

Marcus looked directly at his wife for the first time since he had started talking. He didn't wait for her to reply. He had used the moments before Anne-Marie woke to force himself into his work state, to silence the doubt temporarily. It had been a struggle but his work head was now firmly in place.

Whilst Anne-Marie engaged with his question his gaze shifted as it always did when he was focussed fully on a client. He looked just beyond her shoulders rather than at her face, observing her with a level of acuity and awareness that meant he could see her every response as if it was magnified. She was now fully within his field of vision.

He spoke again, feeling the movements of his tongue inside his mouth, the shaping of his lips, the sounds of the word-vibrations he released.

'In fact we can go even further and say we are good with the process of change and growth and renewal for two reasons that are so very obvious we often fail to acknowledge them consciously. When we do we can use these reasons as a source of comfort and support and power.

'Now, you might wonder what are these two reasons? Well, that is a very good thing to wonder.

'The first reason, as I've already said, is simply the nature of everything. And the nature of everything is constant movement, constant change. Only the conscious mind wants to believe that things are fixed, that there is unmoving stability. The subconscious – the deep well of our most powerful resources including healing – keeps time with the rhythms of nature, the pulse of the planet, the shifts in the seasons, the seeding of new life. The subconscious is the well from which we draw.'

Marcus could see the trance he was building enveloping Anne-Marie. It was soft on her skin as the duvet, inviting her deeper. He let it wrap gently around himself, too; letting his state shift so he could lead the way.

'Sometimes we are well aware of at least part of that process and sometimes we are not aware of it all. And some people ask, "Is it better to be aware or is it better to be unaware?" And the answer is, "It is better to be experiencing it the way you are now. Because your unconscious right now knows how deeply into the well to go.

'Gently and softly. Fathomless. With life at every level. No matter how deep you go. Know matter changing for the better with every breath as you…Just simply…That's right…All the way down…Because we float and sink best when we forget so many things including…The time for us to change for the better is actually timelessness, when we feel the warmth of the support all around us and the weight is taken from us because when there is no time there can be no waiting because everything is forgotten. Had you forgotten that too?

'Well I'm sure it's for the best, and now just so that you can really enjoy how far you are travelling already – and the journey is only just beginning remember, because you might be in danger of forgetting even this – let yourself try gently, impossibly and in vain, to remember whatever it was – or wherever it was – you wondered so long ago, so far away…Sinking ever more deeply as you do…Sinking…'

8

Peter Jones's eyes opened abruptly.

The clock by his side of the bed showed it was 6.50am, ten minutes before the alarm was due to go off. He had suffered another fitful night's sleep.

Peter looked instinctively at his partner, Nic, who lay unmoving with his back turned to him from the far side of their king-size. He saw the now familiar lines of tension in his shoulders. He got the unmistakeable impression again that Nic was feigning sleep. Peter eased out of the bed, complicit in the lie, choosing as he had the day before and the day before that to act as if he had not seen the truth.

He padded out of the room, taking care to close the door quietly behind him.

For as long as he and Nic had been together, Peter had always been the first to rise. He was used to being the person who brought movement into the house each morning, who breathed life into each room.

He had believed for longer than he could remember that for a house to become a home it had to be reinvigorated with the energy of every new day. So each morning as he went from room to room, when he opened the curtains, whilst he waited for the kettle to boil, Peter thought of all the great memories associated with the time he had spent living here with Nic.

Only now the feeling inside him was changing. It was becoming increasingly difficult to focus on reinvigorating the house when he knew their relationship was damaged, possibly fatally so. Now, if there were any obvious threads holding them together they were few and far between.

'Hanging on,' he mused, shivering slightly in the early

morning chill of the kitchen. 'That's the best we are doing right now. That's the damage *it* causes.'

It was the job. It wanted more than just your time. It wanted your energy, your commitment, your willingness to sacrifice. And in return it didn't care if it destroyed you and those closest to you. It was a selfish bastard. It took everything you had day after day and fucked you in return.

It was irresistible.

That was the bottom line.

Peter had been hooked from the very first moment. An immediate addiction. More powerful than any drug. More hypnotic even than the smell of a lover's skin.

Complete.

Pressing you always to let it into your home. To reveal to your family just who you become when you are in its embrace. Pressing always for the opportunity to suffocate everyone else you held dear, to ruin the hearts of those who trusted you with their love.

Peter knew it was only a matter of time before things came to a head between himself and Nic. Whilst this was not his first serious romance it was by far the most meaningful, the closest he had ever been to experiencing what he guessed people meant when they talked of true love.

It *was*.

Already he was thinking of their connection in the past tense. Not because he had lost his love for Nic. Far from it. It was because the great destructive affair had thrust its way into their home, forcing Peter to show what it did to him.

The night that Ethan Hall had been caught Nic had seen the other side of Peter's character for the very first time. He had seen the Detective Chief Inspector, the emotionless, implacable hunter, the man who played the most dangerous of professional games against the most dangerous of opponents. The man who always won.

Nic had seen him, the man who could not escape the harsh embrace of the job.

'I don't want to escape it.' Peter's words came out unplanned.

He heard them in the way he heard a suspect's statement. Cold. Clinical. His mind racing behind an emotionless face to identify all possible connections and implications, going from individual details to big picture and back again in fractions of a second. Hearing what wasn't said as clearly as what was. Knowing that the trick was to keep the suspect talking, to keep asking questions.

'Why don't you quit?' He whispered. 'When you know it's so destructive?'

'Because it's what I do.'

'Is it?'

The answer came quickly. He'd thought it would. Some suspects are desperate to tell the truth. Even if it guarantees a guilty verdict.

'No. It's not what I do. That's the excuse. The lie. It's not what I do. It's what I am. That's why I can't end it yet. I still need to hunt.'

'No matter what the cost?'

'I don't mean to hurt those who love me. That's not my motive.'

'That doesn't absolve you of your guilt.'

'I'm not looking for absolution.'

'Of course you are not. That's how you cope with the damage you cause. You believe it's acceptable as long as you suffer too.'

'There's still a chance for Nic and me. We're still hanging on.'

'We both know you are kidding yourself.'

'No! He's special! Our relationship is not like any of the others!'

'Wasn't it?'

'It isn't over yet!' Peter heard his voice, angry and fearful, as if it wasn't his own. He then realised the kettle had boiled unnoticed and that the mobile phone was buzzing on the worktop like an angry wasp. He put it to his ear.

The news stabbed into his brain and then down through his entire system. His blood automatically pulled away from the extremities of his body and pooled in his core, protecting and supporting his vital organs. His brain fired jolts of adrenaline and cortisol.

Just a few short sentences, just the relaying of one simple fact, and the flight-fight-or freeze state was automatically created, his partner Nic forgotten.

Detective Chief Inspector Jones ended the call without saying a word. He left the kitchen without pouring himself a drink. He walked out of the house in silence. He had to go to work.

Ethan Hall had escaped from the hospital.

9

It had been as easy as Peter feared; as easy as Ethan Hall had known it would be.

The synesthete had lain awake for most of the night. It was hard to sleep when the vivid, multi-coloured future you were about to create was only hours away.

Anticipation had its own distinct colour and shape. It fizzed and flashed like miniature lightning bolts. It brought the taste of copper, the taste of blood, to his mouth. This was especially strong when it merged as it did now with its ideal emotional partner: Certainty.

Anticipation mixed with hope was exciting but, if not managed carefully, it risked tipping into the dull stench of desperation. Anticipation mixed with certainty was something else altogether. Its power made even more so by its rarity. Few were the people who ever genuinely felt the two combine.

From Ethan's perspective anticipation mixed with certainty was more than a human cocktail. It was the power that religious fools gave to their gods. It was Supreme Knowledge. It was control of the future. It was his. He had shared the night with it.

Then he had simply slipped out of the bed, crossed the room, and opened the door.

The police constable had turned abruptly. Ethan placed his right hand high against the doorframe. The constable took a half-pace backwards. Ethan smiled. The constable stopped retreating and returned the smile. 'My name is Patrick,' he said.

The next thing he knew a nurse was easing him back into consciousness. He was laying, almost naked, on the prisoner's bed. Although his mind seemed to be working as normal, his face and body felt distant and uncooperative.

'My name is Doreen,' the nurse said, leaning over him and mouthing the words explicitly. 'Nod if you understand me.' She was a robust, Afro-Caribbean woman who gave the impression she had been through far too much in her life to let panic take an easy hold.

Patrick nodded.

'I've already called for assistance,' she said. 'I've already told them that Ethan has gone. We think he must have walked out of the hospital wearing your police uniform.'

Jesus Christ! I'm responsible for a serial killer escaping! Patrick's thoughts were in sharp, hurtful contrast to the numb disconnect everywhere else.

'How did he do this to you?' Doreen asked. 'Did he inject you with something?'

Patrick shook his head. *How did he do this to me?* His mind raced, crashing almost immediately into a single memory that blocked the rest of his encounter with Ethan. 'Introduth mythelf,' he mumbled.

Doreen straightened and looked down at him. 'Well, this is a new one on me,' she said. 'Your pulse is really strong and, if anything, it indicates that you are in a very relaxed state. It's as if you are just taking your time coming out of a very deep sleep. The question is, what made you go to sleep in the first place?'

Patrick forced his right hand to twitch. Doreen paid it no attention. Instead she checked her watch.

'The cavalry is on its way,' she said with what was meant to be a supportive, understanding smile.

Patrick closed his eyes. Detective Chief Inspector Peter Jones would be leading the cavalry and Patrick was absolutely sure he wasn't coming to his rescue. He feared it would be quite the opposite. He was certain that things would deteriorate even further if he were unable to explain to the DCI just how Ethan Hall had got passed him.

Patrick shook his head from side to side, trying desperately to dislodge his mental roadblock.

Just what the hell had happened?

10

They had shaken hands.

That was what happened just a few seconds after Patrick introduced himself.

Ethan Hall had moved his hand from the doorframe and offered it, open, in time-honoured fashion.

Patrick, still struggling to make sense of why he had felt compelled to introduce himself, had been unable to resist the invitation. His right hand had reached out and, just a split second before it touched Ethan's, the synesthete made his move. His own hand rolled beneath Patrick's, catching the wrist between his thumb and his forefinger, turning the palm in, raising Patrick's hand upwards until it was level with his eyes.

The constable blinked involuntarily. Ethan moved forwards, his left hand reaching out to rest on Patrick's right shoulder. At the same time he moved the captured hand towards Patrick's face.

'Just go all the way down,' he whispered.

Patrick's eyes fluttered and closed, incapable of focussing on the lines of his palm as they rapidly filled his vision. He lost conscious awareness before his hand touched his face.

Now, as Ethan walked calmly along Derby Road towards the city centre, he took a moment to relive his first, truly influential interaction with another human being since the coma caught his fall.

And what an interaction it had been! For the first time in his life, he had wiped another person's short-term memory clear! Now he could influence someone's ability to remember as well as he could their current experience. He could change their perspective and their past, albeit temporarily. Maybe one day, he considered, he would be able to remove someone's memory permanently. It would be a great example of a punishment worse than death. And he already had several such punishments planned. The constable, Ethan told himself, would never know just how significant he was; what a great turning point he represented.

Ethan allowed himself a smile as he strolled past Canning Street police station. Then he allowed himself to remember something else, something altogether different. The thought of Patrick lying helpless on the bed had stirred a distant memory, one he had left untouched for a very long time.

Before he had killed his first human being he had paid a woman to have sex with him.

Sort of.

He had actually wanted to see what it looked like, what it really looked like, when a woman had an orgasm. He had watched pornography; seen the boredom and fakery of the woman in the film, watched her thinking of other things, mundane everyday things, as she let half a dozen men do everything they wanted with her body. He had watched her pretend.

So he had paid a woman to go back to the flat that he had shared with Darren, his very limited drug-dealing, so-called friend. He had told her to make herself come. That was all. She didn't need to do anything to him. She didn't even need to strip if she didn't have to. She just had to lie on his bed and orgasm. Just once. Honestly.

He had even warned her not to fake it. He had stressed to her it would be a grave error to think she could trick him.

'We have a deal,' he said. 'I have given you money to do what I want. I expect you to show me what I've paid for.'

And still the stupid bitch thought he was just like everyone else. She undid her jeans, slipped her right hand inside the black cotton of her panties, closed her eyes and pretended. He watched in silence.

Five minutes.

A pathetic, pathetic, show.

When she stopped moaning and opened her eyes he breathed his anger onto her. He saw the first flicker of doubt cross her face. He fanned it with his next breath. Watched it grow and spread. She gasped. It was genuine this time. She could feel his anger – her doubt – holding her, weighing her down. It took only seconds for her to realise she couldn't move, that she was his prisoner. There were tears in her eyes when he spoke next.

'You agreed to come for me,' he said. 'You promised. I didn't challenge you when you lied about your name. Or when you pretended you'd never had sex for money. I didn't challenge you about those things because I don't care about them, I didn't need you to be honest about them. I only needed you to be honest with your cunt.'

He used the last words like a knife, stabbing them into her. Her pain was exaggerated because she had no way of preparing for it. She writhed in agony, her stomach twisting, whilst her chest, arms and lower legs were pinned to the bed.

He waited until the pain had subsided before he said, 'You're about to tell me I can have my money back if I just let you go. Save your breath. You are going to keep the money and I am going to see what I paid for.'

'No ... No. I can't. Not for real.' She panted the words. 'I'm sorry. I didn't mean to let you down. I just can't do it for you. I'll do anything else! Honestly! Anything. Just not that. Please! I only do that with my boyfriend.'

He nodded. He understood. He really did. Only it made no difference. She should have said, 'No'. Only she hadn't. They had a deal. She had taken his money. Now she was going to deliver her side of the bargain. She was going to come. Even though he wasn't her boyfriend.

'Look at me,' he said.

She did. She had no choice. She didn't know why. She just had to.

'Just remember what he does to you. How he does it. He knows what to do. Right? He knows precisely how to make you come. So, remember now how it feels when he does. Remember the feeling. Feel it start. Inside. Feel the first sensation in your stomach. Hear the first thoughts. You know the thoughts. You know how they just seem to start unbidden. You know how they grow. They grow just like the feeling grows. You know how the feeling grows. How it builds. How it swells and draws you down and makes you forget everything else. How it becomes the only thing you need. Right. Now. Feel it grow. Feel it grow now. You know how. Remember the movements, the breathing, the anticipation...That's right. Good girl.'

It took him only three minutes.

She cried as she came. The tears lasted longest. He didn't wait for them to stop.

After the second time he told her if she had honoured the deal, once would have been enough. Only now it wasn't.

It wasn't nearly enough.

He kept her pinned to the bed for two days. He made her orgasm time after time. Relentlessly. Remorselessly. He watched the colours firing from her body and her mouth as she climaxed. He watched pleasure and embarrassment and shame turn into pain and then agony. He watched fear turn into terror as she realised he could kill her this way.

He watched her body lose control. He watched her lose the fight to control her bladder and her bowels. He watched the storm of emotions on her face as he made her come continually despite her mess. He watched her lose track of time, lose awareness of everything else.

Even when she passed out, her subconscious heard his words and her body responded. He watched how her orgasm dissipated and how its colours changed as she neared death.

For two days he did something to her that her boyfriend never would.

He ruined her.

She was not the first person he killed. Not quite.

He never wondered if she would have preferred to die.

11

Peter Jones strode through the hospital Ethan Hall had walked out of dressed as a policeman trying desperately to focus only on the problem at hand. Trying with every fibre of his being to stop the thoughts of what this might mean to him and Nic, to Marcus and Anne-Marie or anyone else unfortunate enough to be targeted by Ethan Hall.

Peter's face was grim when he stepped into the private room that had once housed a killer. The young constable was still in bed, on doctor's orders. He looked terrified.

I should have insisted they keep two officers on the door.

'Patrick it wasn't your fault.' Peter meant to sound reassuring, but they both heard the criticism in his voice. Only he knew it was directed inwards.

'I'm really sorry, sir.' The confusion in the officer's face was tangible. So was the fear. His eyes were inappropriately wide as if straining to catch a glimpse of something that had vanished mysteriously.

'There's no need to be sorry.' *You didn't stand a chance.* 'You did everything we could have asked of you. And at least it seems your voice is back to normal. I heard you'd been struggling with it.'

'When I first woke up, yes. Then it suddenly came back.'

'Well, that's good. I'm sure everything else will over time. Right now I need to ask you some questions.'

'Of course, sir.' The eyes widened even more. 'It's just that I don't think there's any point in you asking. You see, when I try to think about what happened it's like I keep falling into a hole in my mind. I can remember seeing him standing there. And his smile. And his hand. And then it just stops. There's nothing. Nothing until I saw the nurse. And then my entire body felt the way your mouth does when you're at the dentist. Do you know what I mean, sir?'

'Of course.'

Patrick's eyes moistened. 'To be honest sir, I feel useless.' He blinked repeatedly. Tears began to flow. He wiped his eyes with the back of his hand. *Keeping it masculine*, Peter thought. 'Can he really have, you know, done something to me? Got in my head in some way that I'll never get rid of?'

'You are going to be all right. As you said, it's like being at the dentist's. It'll wear off.'

'So the memory will come back? I will be able to help?'

'You're helping already. Just sharing how you are feeling is useful. Ethan Hall is a very unusual man, so every little scrap of information is important. And I'm sure your memory will return.'

'What if it doesn't?'

Treat it is as a blessing. 'It won't be a great loss to our case. Ethan has escaped from police custody, that's all that matters. It will be another thing to add to the list of charges he's going to answer for.'

'Why didn't he kill me?'

'He's not a mindless murderer. He's more concerned with making a point, leaving an imprint, being acknowledged. That's what he's making us do now – we're acknowledging how he managed to get away. And to be honest with you Patrick, he'd sooner have you wondering and worrying about how he affected your memory than simply dead. Just about anyone can kill if they're pushed enough. He's reminding us that he's different from the rest.'

'So how do we beat him?'

'We are the biggest and best team in the land. One way or another we always win. That's why you joined, right?'

'Yes, sir!' Patrick's cheeks showed a hint of colour for the first time since Peter's arrival. 'And I want to get out of here as soon as possible. I want to get back to work!'

The Detective Chief Inspector stood up and let his chest swell slightly as he nodded his encouragement. Secretly his mind was racing. If Ethan Hall had permanently erased Patrick's memory of their encounter, if he really could do that, how the hell did they get any new witnesses? How long would it take to track him down if no one could remember seeing him, if no one could report what he said or did? Could the synesthete possibly have more power than he or Marcus had realised? Dear God ...

Despite the terrifying new possibility, Peter Jones maintained his confident exterior. 'Don't worry, Patrick,' he said. 'We'll have you back in uniform in no time. Believe me.'

12

Ethan Hall had disposed of his police jacket, tie and cap within a hundred metres of leaving the hospital. He had opened the shirt collar and rolled up the sleeves. To anyone who gave him a casual glance he didn't look like a policeman anymore. He didn't walk like one either. Thus, he was able to stroll through the Meadows estate without attracting any undue attention from those he passed.

Darren, the drug-addict waster who thought they were friends, had moved into a two-bedroomed end of terraced house. He still swam down amongst the lowest dredges of society. He still thought he mattered.

Ethan's nostrils flared instinctively as he turned off the pavement towards Darren's front door. The air wasn't the best out here, far from it. But it was a damn sight better than inside Darren's house.

Ethan breathed in deeply as he took the last few steps before knocking on the door. His peripheral vision clocked Darren's pale, thin face staring briefly through the lounge window. Then he closed down eighty per cent of his olfactory system as the door opened and he stepped inside without being asked.

'Fuck me, mate!' Darren backed off automatically. His skin paled even more than normal. His breathing was high in his chest. When he had last spent time with Ethan he had regarded him as a harmless weirdo. He had enjoyed his companionship because he had felt superior. After all, he was the one with the contacts. The man who could scare most law-abiding people because he was at least one step across the line and could exaggerate that fact to anyone who didn't know any better. Now Darren had a very different perspective of the man who had walked into his lounge as if he owned the place. Now everyone knew who Ethan Hall was. At least they knew what he had done – even if there were a whole range of different stories going round about how he had actually done it.

Darren locked his front door and followed the killer into his front room. He couldn't help but glance twice at the trousers he was wearing. He forced the question back down his throat. He was sure that Ethan Hall was smiling at him even though his face hadn't even twitched. For some reason he found that almost as frightening as staring down the barrel of a gun.

'Ethan. Fuck me mate!' Darren said it again because it was an easy way to make himself breathe out and because he really didn't know what else to say without putting himself at risk.

'Darren. You haven't changed.'

Ethan Hall said that. He definitely said that because Darren heard it loud and clear. Even though he hadn't seen Ethan's face move.

'No mate. I'm er...Well, you know how it is.' Darren said that. Definitely. He heard his own voice. He was just struggling to feel any connection with his mouth. It was as if he was suddenly locked in a place way behind his lips. He could tell they were moving, but it felt as if they were distanced and cold. It was, he realised, a bit like how you felt after the dentist had injected you, only far, far stronger. And much worse. At least with the dentist you expected it and eventually you felt better because of it. Ethan Hall didn't do things to make people feel better. That much Darren was sure of. He bit his lower lip. He felt nothing. Ethan smiled again.

'Yes. I know how it is.' Ethan sat down on the brown corduroy two-seater settee. He didn't seem to notice the stains on it. Darren remained standing. Glued to the spot. 'That's why I am here,' Ethan said, 'because I know how it is, because you are the man who knows the people with power. You know what I mean?'

Darren nodded. His head felt heavy and numb.

'Of course you do. That's because you have your finger on the pulse. You've seen the news, haven't you?'

Darren nodded again.

'Do you believe I killed those people?'

'Uhm...' The question created a tingle of sensation, like a mild electric shock, that buzzed from the back of Darren's head to his lips. Just what was the right answer? And what was the consequence for getting it wrong?

'Don't be afraid, Darren. Tell me the truth.'

Easier said than done. Darren bit his lip again. He gasped as he tasted blood. He staggered back a pace, remembering suddenly the crazy, unbelievable story about Ethan Hall that he had heard some years before.

A part-time hooker had whispered to one of her friends that Ethan had abused her in the most bizarre of ways, had kept her prisoner and damaged her without even touching her. Her friend had whispered it to someone else who had whispered it to Darren. He had dismissed it as the drug-addled ramblings of a tart with no idea of who did what to her from one day to the next. But now, since the publicity about Ethan Hall, since the stories in the media, he wondered if it was true. After all if he could scalp you, cut the top of your head off without you feeling any pain, surely he could do anything?

'C'mon, Darren. Answer the question.'

'Well, it, er, didn't actually say in the news that ya'd killed people. It wasn't anything definite, y'know what I mean? It was just that you'd been arrested in connection with, y'know, some murders. And ya can't believe everythin' you 'ear in the news, can ya?'

'And?'

'And I, er, I think you can do things the rest of us can't understand.'

'How right you are.' Ethan scratched his nose with the forefinger of his right hand. Darren saw it all clearly. Suddenly his senses were working normally again.

'How, how can I help you mate?' It seemed the best way to move things on. Ethan Hall was a wanted man. Even he would need people to do things for him now.

Unless he could hypnotise every copper in the country to turn a blind eye.

Somehow that thought made Darren feel even worse. Which was ridiculous given that he hated the police, given that if he had the courage he would kill one himself. At least with them, though, he knew what he was dealing with.

'You can help me by setting up a meeting.'

'Sure. Of course. Anything you say. Who do you want to meet?'

'Calvin.'

Darren blinked. 'You want to see Calvin?'

'Yeah.'

'Are you sure, mate? I mean –'

'I'm certain.' Ethan raised his right hand, his palm facing Darren. The movement rather than the words silenced Darren completely, robbed him of any desire to speak. 'I am always certain,' Ethan said. 'Right now I'm certain you will do as I tell you, and I'm telling you to arrange a meeting. Understand?'

Darren nodded.

'Good.' Ethan lowered his hand. 'So make the call. I want to see the Numbers Man.'

13

Anne-Marie was struggling to keep her secret. It was a secret about the numbers. She was struggling to keep it in, in the way she had struggled – and failed – to keep the contents of her stomach in on so many occasions in the last few months. In the way she was struggling and failing to keep her emotions in.

The callous irony gripping her tight was simply this: she was struggling to keep everything in apart from the one thing she most needed to get out. And that wasn't going anywhere.

In fact, it was growing.

The numbers don't lie.

That was the cold, hard fact her doctors had shared with her. Her cancer was growing, spreading. She was struggling to keep other things in because they all wanted to escape the cancer invasion. The rest of her – body and mind – was behaving now like the displaced peoples she had seen on TV, forced to flee from irresistible attack.

Why does your body do this to itself?

Anne-Marie has asked herself that question a thousand times. Somehow she had created her own killing mechanism even though she wanted to live forever. Or at least into a very old age and certainly until Marcus died.

Marcus...

She hadn't yet told him that her condition was worsening. A part of her didn't want to tell him. She didn't want to see the look on his face when he realised he was failing to save her. The rest of her, though, was desperate for her to speak, to give herself – to give him – the chance to fight back, to regain the lost ground. After all, even displaced people returned to their homeland.

Sometimes.

Once the enemy had been driven out. That was the determining factor. It didn't matter if everything had been destroyed, every homeland could be rebuilt as long as there was no more internal fighting. Over time it could become even better than it used to be, more suited to the present, more relevant, more courageous.

And her body was like her homeland, wasn't it? Because the notion of homeland was more than just the place where you lived. It was as much historical and emotional as it was tangible and current. Homeland was just a body of land influenced by a range of forces, just as her physical self was. Homeland had its own boundaries that you sought to control just as you sought to control the boundaries to your physical self. Homeland was open to invasion, no matter how hard you tried to prevent it, just as your body was.

Cancer: an internal terrorist.

That was her enemy and, like all terrorists, it was brilliant at disguising itself and spreading silently, making itself known only when it was strong enough to cause serious harm. An internal terrorist feeding on her homeland, robbing her of her most precious resources, threatening to drive everything else out.

Anne-Marie was standing in the bedroom of their rented house, looking out at the valley. It made her long for the willow tree that dominated the garden of the real home they had left behind. She loved that tree. She always had. There was something about the way it grew out of the earth, reached for the sky and returned to the land with the most gentle sweep and touch. In her mind the willow tree represented something beyond itself, something more; something that offered hope beyond the pain and fear and doubt of everyday experience.

Only she had chosen to walk away from the willow tree. As if by changing location you can leave bad things behind. As if you can escape from yourself, your memories and your cancer, by simply changing house. That, of course, was nonsense. It didn't matter where you went or how far you travelled, you could never escape the influence of your homeland. When all else was stripped away, you and it were inseparable.

Just like her and Marcus.

Inseparable.

For better or worse.

14

Numbers destroyed doubt.

That was what Calvin Brent believed.

He believed in the power of numbers. If the numbers added up, everything was good. Numbers were a form of truth that couldn't be denied. Two plus two equalled four. Four plus four equalled eight. And so on and so on. The more money you made, the richer you were. The more people you killed the more power you had. Especially when the right people knew about it.

Any way you looked at it numbers were the ultimate measure and since he had been in charge, since his dad had been put away courtesy of that scumbag Peter Jones, everything was adding up better than ever before.

Now Calvin Brent sat back in his chair, looked at his unexpected visitor, and tried to make sense of just what was going on. He tried to make two and two equal four. He tried to make the numbers add up. For the first time he was struggling to make it happen. He kept his face stone cold and emotionless. He knew that sooner or later the numbers would fall into line.

'So,' Ethan Hall said, 'the bottom line is I can help you if you help me.'

Calvin Brent had followed the Ethan Hall media story with a mixture of fascination and bewilderment. Darren was, and always had been, the most minor sort of player in Brent's world. He was an amoeba in a sea filled with sharks. Yet Brent did not dismiss people like Darren as easily as others did – as easily as his father had. Calvin was the Numbers Man. He knew that everything grew out of the lowest common denominator. He knew that a million was just the term used to describe a collection of many smaller things joined together. Big things were the result of controlling and bringing together a wide range of amoeba to create a powerful whole. Amoeba were the building blocks of power.

So Calvin had never been dismissive of Darren, but neither had he any desire to turn him into something more. He served the Numbers Man just fine as he was: the smallest fraction in a most complicated sum.

Calvin had been surprised, then, when, as Ethan Hall's fame grew, Darren started spreading it around that they were big mates. If the stories about Hall were even half true, he was clearly a big fish – a most unusual big fish – and such creatures didn't buddy-up with amoeba. Yet just one hour ago Darren had called him saying that not only had Ethan Hall escaped from police custody, he actually wanted a meeting. Calvin couldn't help but wonder if Darren had been taking too much of the stuff he should have been selling, but he said 'Yes' on the off-chance. And the calculated gamble had paid off.

Numbers, Calvin thought, *they rule the world.*

Only as he looked at Ethan Hall, things were not quite adding up.

'I don't doubt that I could help you if I chose to,' he said finally, 'but I don't see any way you can be of use to me.'

'Haven't you read the papers or watched the TV?' Ethan's lips curled into what was either a smile or a snarl, Calvin couldn't tell. In fact he realised he was struggling to process anything at his usual speed. He took confidence, though, from the fact that his confusion was well hidden behind his poker face. And he was an outstanding poker player. No one beat him. Ever.

'You know who I am, right?' Calvin didn't wait for an answer. 'You're a freak the police have already grabbed once. I'm a professional and I've never been arrested. I have contacts that stretch from here to the other side of the world. You're on your own. You're wanted and isolated and out of your depth. All the numbers are on my side. So don't come to me thinking you're someone special.'

'I wasn't thinking.' Ethan's lips curled again. 'I was looking.'

'And?'

'We should play cards sometime. You would find it an experience. Now,' Ethan clapped his hands once, 'suppose I show you just how special I am, make you realise how I can actually help you, and then tell you what I need in return.'

Calvin wanted to be angry. He wanted to call in one of the guys to slap the freak's face off his shoulders, maybe break a few bones, and see how smug he was then. Only he couldn't feel the emotion. He couldn't feel anything. He just heard himself say, 'I'll give you one chance.'

'Of course you will.' Ethan looked around the room as if something was missing and then said, 'I can make people do things. I can make them do anything in fact. Bring one of your boys in and give him a gun. I'll show you how very special I am.'

'Matt!' The shout was out of Calvin's mouth in an instant, as if released automatically by Ethan's words. Within seconds a burly, shaven-headed man wearing black jeans and a black tee shirt came through the door.

'Boss?'

'I need you for an experiment.' Calvin reached into his desk drawer and took out a heavy, black pistol. Matt looked from it to his boss and then across to Ethan.

'Here,' Calvin offered the weapon. The large man took it slowly. He kept his finger well away from the trigger.

'Face me,' Ethan ordered.

The man did as he was told. His eyes locked onto Ethan's.

'Raise the gun and point it at my face.'

It took less than a second.

'Good. Now wrap your finger around the trigger as if you are going to try to shoot me. Let's have no waiting around, no reason to guard against this now Matt. Don't make this difficult or impossible for yourself now, just try it.'

Ethan took a pace forwards as he spoke. Matt's forearm flexed as he tried to squeeze the trigger. His arm tensed but his finger didn't move. He grunted as if he was struggling to lift a heavy weight. Nothing happened. Matt glanced towards Calvin. He redoubled his effort. Sweat beaded his face. His hand began to shake. Ethan laughed, harsh and abrupt. Matt's gun hand stilled. Ethan turned away from him and faced the crime boss.

'So ...' Ethan paused deliberately, '...that was part one of the lesson.'

Calvin shook his head. He still didn't feel as alert as normal but he knew what he had just seen. 'All you've taught me is that you couldn't make Matt do what you told him to.'

'No. He did exactly what I told him to. You just didn't see it. Or hear it. Or understand it. You will understand this, though.'

Ethan returned his attention to Matt. He took another step forwards. He spoke in the calm, reassuring tone of a parent soothing their child. 'Now, looking at me closely, just take the pistol and put it in your mouth.'

Calvin Brent watched in amazement as the man he paid to intimidate and beat others opened his mouth and put the gun barrel in as far as it would go.

It's like he's sucking cock.

Brent realised he was staring open-mouthed. He pulled back in his chair and clamped his mouth shut.

Ethan smiled reassuringly as Matt's lips closed around the metal. 'Let me tell you what you are going to do,' he said. 'You are going to squeeze the trigger very, very slowly until the gun fires and blows your brains out. Do you understand?'

Matt nodded.

Calvin's vision folded inwards, focussing only on Matt's trigger finger. It grew large in his mind's eye, blotting out everything else. He saw the pressure increase. Bit by bit.

He heard Ethan Hall whisper, 'Good boy.'

He saw Matt's finger increase its pressure. The trigger began to depress. It was all happening in slow motion. The result was inevitable. Another fraction of an inch and Matt's head was going to explode. He was going to do what Ethan Hall had said! How could that be possible? Another split-second passed. The movement was almost complete. Calvin realised that Matt was staring, unblinking at Ethan. He realised the hypnotist had no intention of saving his life.

'Stop it!' Calvin roared at the top of his voice. 'Stop it now!'

Matt staggered as if struck. It looked to Calvin as if he was suddenly, for the first time, aware of what he had been about to do. Matt pulled the gun from his mouth and began to retch violently. Ethan Hall didn't wait for him to stop.

'Now do you see? Was that obvious enough for you? I can make people do anything. I can stop them from pulling the trigger just as easily as I can make them take their own life. Think about that. Just think what I could do for you.'

Calvin Brent nodded slowly. Thinking was currently proving even more difficult than before. If he hadn't seen it with his own eyes he would never have believed what had just happened. But he had seen it. Ethan Hall was unique. He was just the man he needed to solve a problem that had been troubling him.

'What do you want from me?' Calvin asked.

'There are some people I need to find.'

'You just want some addresses?'

'And a driver to get me to them.'

'And for that you are prepared to do me a favour?'

'Yes.'

Brent nodded again, deliberately this time, as if weighing up the odds, as if he needed to really think about this. His poker face was inscrutable.

'How many people?'

'Less than a handful.'

Brent held his silence for a few seconds before replying. He was vaguely aware of Matt standing motionless on one side of the room. 'What I'd want in return for that is non-negotiable. I need someone to die. I need it to be a natural death. Do you understand?'

Ethan didn't flinch. 'I can make that happen.'

'Let me be really clear – I don't need it to look like a natural death; I need it to be a natural death. Are you sure you can make that happen?'

'Of course. Especially if you can answer a few questions about the person concerned.'

'What sort of questions?'

'Nothing to do with your relationship with them; just personal stuff that will let me work out how to create what you want.'

'I thought you'd be able to work it all out for yourself once you got there.' Brent leaned forward on his desk. He couldn't help but wonder if this was the first chink he'd seen in the other man's armour. 'Or are you not quite as good as you make out?'

'Trust me, I'm better than that. I just thought you'd like to know in advance what I'm going to do. I thought you'd like the power of knowing everything. I thought you'd want it to be quick and easy, given that you're such a professional.' Ethan's face was expressionless. 'Although I can take a long time over it if that's what you want. Make it messy. Make a lot of noise. Gamble that nobody hears anything. Let the cards fall where they may, so to speak.'

'Don't push your fucking luck.' Calvin forced a scowl; with Matt watching he had no choice but assert his authority, even if it still didn't feel as right and easy as normal. 'You'll get the answers you want, then just make it look like an act of God.'

'It'll be the nearest thing.'

'Yeah, right.'

'You'll see. Whoever your target is, they are as good as dead already.'

Calvin nodded, his mind racing, his thoughts coming back under his control. *Never play the cards, play the man*, his father had told him. *And always plan ahead.* Ethan Hall certainly warranted some precise and cautious planning, and he already knew too much to be allowed to walk away once his work was done. Calvin nodded again. 'Then we have a deal,' he said.

'I thought we would.' Ethan had watched the change in Brent's skin tone and breathing pattern as he considered his options. He had watched the pupils in his eyes dilate as he imagined what would happen. No matter what he thought, the criminal was actually as obvious as an open book. He waited the few seconds it took for Brent to realise the next question.

'These people you want me to find, what are you going to do with them?'

'I'm going to say a few words.'

Despite the feeling of normality that had just returned – or, perhaps, because of it – Calvin Brent, the Numbers Man, the great poker player, heard those words and shuddered. Until a few minutes ago he had never considered just how much influence one person could exert over another through what they said. He had always relied on muscle to make sure the numbers were right. However, the man standing in front of him had something more powerful than muscle, something far more dangerous, something seemingly irresistible.

Calvin Brent could not imagine – and, truth be told, he didn't care – just what Ethan Hall was going to do to the people he planned to talk to. Whatever it was, it would be both compelling and terrible. Of that he had no doubt.

PART 2

FEAR

15

Did you really think I'd forgotten you?

Did you think that because I hadn't spoken to you directly for a while you were no longer in my mind? Or that I was no longer in yours?

Did you?

Are you really that stupid?

Or are you just that hopeful?

It's what the herd calls Wishful Thinking. It's what they do every time they buy a Lottery ticket. Every time they feel the pain or see the blood and choose not to go to the Doctor's. Every time they say, 'For better or worse' and expect only better. Every time they think 'Better late than never' and believe it will be.

Wishful Thinking.

Just one of the reasons why I have no sympathy or respect for you. One of the many reasons.

So let's be clear about this: you have brought this on yourselves. It didn't have to involve so many of you. It could have been just between me and him. And if you had let me just put him properly in his place it would have taken a stain out of your world, too. Only you have your rules and your false allegiances, based on habit and fear and expectation. You have your beliefs. They make you cling. And when you cling to a sinking ship you drown. Simple as.

So you can practice as much deep breathing as you want. It won't make any difference. The depths I am going to take you to will burst your heart. Every heart. Everyone of you.

It is all mapped out. From the moment I opened my eyes it was laid out before me.

Like a red carpet. At once a reflection of my special status and a marking of the way forward. And like every red carpet my plan runs into a very particular place. And like every red carpet only a chosen few ever get to the end of it.

And the ones I have chosen will realise eventually they have reached the worst of all possible endings. Each individually created. Bespoke, specific and tailored.

After all, I'm not the only one who's here to serve.

16

Liam Hemsall couldn't stop himself thinking about the day – that special day – when he had spoken the oath. It seemed such a long time ago now. The images in his mind's eye were blurred and hazy. The words, though, they were as clear as a bell. They still rang out. Which, he guessed, was why he couldn't stop repeating them in his mind.

'I do solemnly and sincerely declare that I will well and truly serve the Queen in the office of constable, with fairness, integrity, diligence and impartiality, upholding fundamental human rights and according equal respect to all people...'

I will well and truly serve...

That was the motivating factor. It always had been. The desire to serve, to use his authority, skill and judgement for the benefit of society. Liam didn't know where the urge first came from. He hadn't grown up in a family of police officers. He hadn't been inspired by the ever-increasing number of tv dramas that sought to find a new spin on the cops and robbers theme. And he certainly hadn't been drawn to the idea of wearing a uniform. No, for some inexplicable reason he had grown up coming to the realisation that the best way to meet his own inherent desire was to join the force. So he had, at the first available opportunity.

And as soon as he'd developed enough general experience he had applied to become part of an Armed Response Team. If you were serious about serving, he reasoned, you needed to be at the sharp end. You needed to be there when you were most needed. You needed to have specialist skills. You needed to be willing to shoulder the biggest responsibilities.

He had sailed through the interview and the subsequent

firearms training. Within a month, as the result of a sudden vacancy, he had found himself a bone fide member of an Armed Response Team. He had felt at home from the very first day.

'Professionally speaking.'

'Why do you feel the need to clarify?'

'Because you can feel at home in different places and with different people without them being your real home or real family. My wife and daughters have a place in my heart that no-one else can touch.'

'It's all a matter of degree?'

'Yes.' Liam swallowed. His throat was dry. His gaze, he realised, had gone down to the floor again, just as it always did whenever he was forced back to this point, to that moment in time.

'Service is a matter of degree too, isn't it?' The psychologist was unbelievably still. He was the only person Liam had ever seen who could question and listen with absolute stillness.

'Yes. Everything is a matter of degree.'

'Even life and death?'

'I didn't kill anyone.'

'I was just asking you to pursue your line of thinking.'

'You talk of thinking as if it's separate from feeling.' Liam eyeballed his questioner. He was grateful to have a reason to look up from the floor. 'You talk about something you've never experienced as if you understand what it means, as if you know the effects it has.'

'My purpose, as you know, is to help you create, acknowledge and then manage your state. I'm only here because you are.'

'I'm only here because I shot someone.'

'And?'

Liam felt like an alcoholic desperate to drink. 'And because he didn't die. And now he's free.'

'He wasn't free when we first met.'

'No.'

'At that time he was expected to die.'

'Yes.'

'You were coming to terms with potentially having killed someone.'

'Struggling to come to terms.'

The psychologist inclined his head. It seemed to Liam that it was at once an acknowledgement and an invitation. He kept talking.

'In fact, as you helped me realise, I was struggling as much with my emotional response to the shooting as with the actual incident.'

'As far as we know, we are the only species capable of having thoughts about our thoughts and feelings about our own feelings. Sometimes when we go meta to our original state we make things worse for a while, not better. So the question is...'

'How much worse is it getting?' Liam finished the psychologist's sentence.

'That's almost the question. Although in that form it does encourage another question.

'Which is?'

What's the *it* you are referring to?'

Liam glanced down. The dull barely recognisable voice in the back of his head whispered, *The pull of the floor, that's what I'm referring to. Pull, pull, pull.*

'It's me.'

'That's right.'

Pause. The psychologist didn't blink. Liam felt as if he was being drawn down into the smallest space, crushed, in danger of being lost forever. He had to speak.

'It was my job, my role, what I had trained for. The situation demanded that I fire my weapon. There shouldn't have been any…'

'Emotional consequences?'

Liam nodded. 'It means I'm not fit for purpose.'

'And yet we are all emotional beings. Our brains are designed for us to feel emotion before we rationalise. All humans – even police officers tasked with carrying and using firearms – are emotional first and foremost. How can feeling a mix of emotions after being obliged to discharge your weapon make you unfit for purpose? Don't you think that if you didn't feel an emotional response it would suggest you were unwell, not the opposite?'

Liam sat back in his chair, the weight of the questions, tangible, pressing against his chest. He managed to say, 'It depends on the emotions.'

'And the emotions we feel about our emotions.' The psychologist glanced down at the floor; at the place Liam was trying so hard to resist. 'Does it mean anything else about you?'

'It means that I don't know who I am, that I never have.'

'And when you were told that he was going to live?'

'I was conflicted. Some part of me was relieved. Some other part said I was a failure.'

'And when you heard that he'd escaped?'

Liam shook his head angrily as if an insect was buzzing and trying to settle on his face. He had received a phone call within hours of Ethan leaving the hospital. He had been warned that for a couple of days at least the press would be all over the story. 'There are no words.'

'In that case, what fills that space?'

'Where the words should be?'

'Yes.'

I do. Pull, pull pull.

Liam shook his head again. 'When you lose something that important nothing can take its place. It's like an earthquake inside you. There's only debris.'

'Rebuilding usually takes time.'

'It's never the same, though.'

'Sometimes it's better.'

'I don't believe it can be. Not in this case. If I'd hit my target, Ethan Hall would be dead. It would be over. At least for everyone else. Now God alone knows what he will do. And it's all because of me.'

'It's because of many other factors, too.'

Liam couldn't look the psychologist in the face. Instead he gave in to his need to share the memory pressing against the front of his head.

'I remember, I hadn't been on the force long and I was having a beer with some of the other lads and DCI Peter Jones came in. I'd heard about him, this great detective who always found a way – Jonah, they called him – and he came over and spent a couple of minutes with us. I remember asking him why he'd become a copper. He didn't hesitate; he just smiled and said, "Because I care about the world." That was it! It was everything I believed and had committed my life to in one simple sentence. He didn't even say it like it was anything clever. To him it was just a statement of fact. He cared about the world and had found the best way to show it. And he hasn't failed yet.'

'How do you know?'

'His record speaks for itself.'

'To a certain degree.'

Liam snorted, 'You're just using my words against me.'

'I'm just using your words. That's not the same thing.'

'Then maybe I'm using my words against me.'

'Maybe you are.'

'Can't you ever give a straight answer to a straight question?'

'You didn't ask a question.'

'Ok. Here's one – who am I?

The psychologist inhaled briefly before he answered. When he did, he looked Liam directly in the eyes. 'I'll tell you exactly who you are,' he said.

17

'You're a fucking incompetent!' Peter Jones stabbed his right forefinger towards the chest of the seated Duty Inspector whose meeting he had just interrupted and ended prematurely. 'Of the highest fucking order!'

'You can't talk to me like that!' Barry Smithson bridled, struggling visibly to regain his composure.

'You're not listening are you? Even though I'm standing right in front of you and talking loudly enough for the rest of the building to hear!'

'Of course I'm – '

Peter stopped the sentence dead in its tracks. He wasn't here for a conversation. 'I can tell you're not listening because I am, in fact, talking to you like that. Listen more closely this time and see if you can spot it – you're a fucking incompetent! And because of your decision to take one of those officers away from Ethan Hall's hospital room – a decision you chose to make even though I explicitly told you we needed two officers there at all times no matter what happened elsewhere – because of your decision, the man I know to be the most dangerous individual I have ever arrested is out there somewhere, free to do whatever he chooses!

'Are you listening to me now? Are you taking more notice than you did when I told you to prioritise keeping two coppers outside that hospital door? Are you starting to understand the magnitude of your arrogant mistake?'

'It … It wasn't arrogance.'

'You chose to ignore me! You – you! – decided I was wrong! You made the deliberate decision to do the precise opposite of what a senior officer told you to do! You did this, no fucker else!' Peter paused, taking a deliberate breath, using the brief silence to increase the pressure, managing and directing his very real anger with deliberation. Now it was time to lower his voice, to condense the emotion. 'So, tell me Barry, who's going to clean your mess up? Eh? Who's going to appease the Superintendent, front the media, reassure the people of Nottingham? Who's gonna catch him again Barry? Is it you?' Peter leaned forward, resting both hands on the desk that separated them. His voice dropped to little more than a whisper. He didn't need to shout anymore. Everyone else had seen and heard enough. The story of this interaction would spread just as he needed it to, a quick and powerful reminder that you didn't ignore Jonah's instructions. 'Is it going to be you, Barry?' He asked again. 'Or is that person going to be me?'

'It's going to be you,' Barry's voice was as low as his gaze.

'Too fucking right.' Peter straightened. 'And I suggest you keep your fingers crossed that I get him before some poor unfortunate in Nottingham pays an unnecessary price.'

'Why...Why are you so sure he'll stay here?'

'Three reasons, if you must know. One, he's a loner. He doesn't have anyone to help him. Two, he's not a professional at this sort of thing. So without real criminal advice he won't be able to move far without us spotting him. And three...' Peter's voice trailed off. This time his hesitation was not a deliberate ploy to stress the other man; this time it was something altogether different. He felt the fear twist and tug in his stomach. 'Three, I know this man. I've had an insight into his mind, into his motives. He won't try to leave the city – at least not for a while yet. He's got unfinished business.'

18

Ethan Hall was finding it almost impossible to ignore the stench inside Darren's house. He managed it as well as he could by treating it as a training exercise in attention management, by focussing on something else or nothing at all. 'If you can control your sense of smell, you can control any aspect of yourself,' he murmured, gazing at the filthy lounge carpet and letting his mind wander back to the night he had almost killed Marcus Kline, particularly to the sound, sight and feeling of the two bullets penetrating his chest.

The memory was broken by Darren opening the front door. His stink preceded him. 'I've got it, mate.' Darren was talking even before he was in the room. 'What you've been waiting for. From Calvin Brent himself. Look. Message in a bottle.' He grinned, gap-toothed and proud of his offering.

'It's an envelope, not a bottle.'

Darren shrugged. 'Just a saying, mate. That's all.' He handed it over and then stepped back a pace, shifting his weight awkwardly from one foot to the other.

'Sit down. Tell me precisely what happened.'

Darren sat. 'I met up with one CB's boys – a big fella, called Matt –'

'– I know him.'

'Do you? Oh, well, he didn't say.'

'No.'

Ethan's smile barely slit his face. It made Darren think of a cut made by a stiletto just a fraction of a second before the blood started leaking. He couldn't help but scratch the scar on the palm of his left hand. 'So, er, so he gave me the envelope, told me it was private business between you and the boss.'

'Is that all he said?'

'Pretty much.'

'Then that isn't all he said, is it?'

The smile seemed to harden before it disappeared.

'The only other thing was that I had to act, you know, as the go-between from now on.'

'Between me and Brent?'

'Between you and them, yeah. To be honest mate, you won't get near CB again. That's not how it works. He always keeps his distance. Truth be told, you did better than most getting to meet him in the first place. No, it'll be Matt I meet with.'

'Unless I tell you otherwise.'

'Yeah. Well, sure. But there'll be no need for that will there? I mean, you've got all the info in there, right?' Darren gestured towards the envelope on Ethan's lap.

'How do you know what's in here?'

'I don't really. It's just that Matt told me there was everything you'd need and you'd know what to do once you'd read it. He said 'e'd see you t'morrow.'

'He said that?' Ethan straightened.

'Yeah. 'E said 'e was gonna be yo'r driver for the next couple of days. Didn't seem too 'appy about it, t'be 'onest with ya.'

'Why didn't you tell me that in the first place?'

'Because I figured you already knew! C'mon mate, I'm doing my best 'ere! I'm on your side, you know that!'

'Of course I do.' Ethan looked at the envelope as he spoke. 'Make sure it's the side you stay on.' He used his right forefinger to pry open the sealed flap and took out the folded sheet of paper. It took less than a second to read. It was not the list of addresses he'd asked for. Instead there was just one blunt directive from Calvin Brent. One sentence. One instruction.

Be ready for pick-up at 10am.

The crime boss was making a point, showing him who was in control. Ethan stared at the sheet of paper; wished it were a face.

A few feet away, Darren recoiled from the sudden cold rush of emotion flooding the room. He pushed himself back into his stained corduroy armchair. It was a futile gesture. There was no escape. No high-ground. For a second, crazily, he was sure he was drowning.

Ethan felt his rage pulsing against his skin. He let it grow. Wordless. A violent meditation. A silent promise. He rode it back to the shore. And realised Darren was holding his breath.

'I wonder why Matt's not too happy about being my driver?' Ethan couldn't keep the smirk from his face. He didn't wonder at all. Matt would still be reliving the fact that he'd come within a heartbeat of putting a bullet through his own brain. He'd be terrified, and pretending to his boss that he wasn't. Calvin Brent, on the other hand, was a fool. He was a fool for showing his hand so brazenly. He was a fool for not being afraid. He was a fool for giving him Matt again. But, then, Ethan reflected, it didn't really matter who his driver was. He would own them regardless.

'I, er, I dunno why 'e's feelin' that way mate.' Darren managed to breathe out an answer. 'I'd of thought it was just a normal job fer 'im, all in a day's work if y'know what I mean? After all, why should it be anythin' else?'

'Why indeed?' Ethan imagined fresh, garden air and inhaled deeply.

'Tha's right!' Darren nodded enthusiastically. 'It'll just be a straight-forward thing, 'course it will. And once you're done, I reckon Matt 'll fill CB in on all the details, I'll report back what he says and we'll all be quids in.'

'There'll be nothing to report back. I'm not one of Brent's lackeys. We have a business deal and once the business is done, the deal is over. Then…' Ethan looked up at the grimy ceiling, '…we're both free to pursue our own agendas.'

'I know what you're saying mate. I really do. It's just that CB decides when the business is over. People don't tell him. He tells them. I'm only saying, 'cos, you know, you're my mate an' that.'

'I'm not *people*.'

'Course not.' Darren swallowed.

'Then make sure you remember it. It's just like you said, I can do things no one else can. So the one thing you can be sure of *mate*, is that it'll be crystal clear to everyone – including him – when my business is finished. Do you understand?'

'Yeah. Sure. Whatever you say.'

'That's right. That's always how it is. It's always whatever I say.' The smile returned abruptly, wider this time, open like a wound.

Darren squeezed his left hand until it hurt.

19

The world was pressing in from every direction. That's how it felt. As if there was a critical mass surrounding him, tightening its grip, providing an unrelenting three-hundred-and-sixty-degree compression without the slightest indication of an escape route or shelter.

For the first time ever, Marcus Kline was finding himself lost for words. The pressure wasn't just taking his breath away it was taking his words also, inside and out. He was struggling to think clearly. He was struggling to speak with skill and authority. The cracks Ethan had caused in his confidence and sense of superiority, cracks he had barely been able to cope with, were suddenly spreading and widening at an alarming speed.

'The structure of your own identity,' he said as if talking to a client rather than himself, 'that very structure is in danger of falling apart. And if it goes...'

His voice stopped as the words disappeared, leaving him once again with only an awareness – even that more like shadows in a fog than his once taken for granted clarity – of the frightening internal emptiness beyond his control.

Marcus kept walking. It was 9.30am. The early morning city rush was over. The streets were still relatively busy, but most people who came here to work were already hard at it. Marcus, disoriented by the fog, was able – just – to steer a path without bumping accidently into anyone. Once upon a time, and it seemed a very long time ago, he had welcomed the bustle and energy of a crowded street. It had been one of his many playgrounds. A place to observe, read and influence others. Now he was incapable of giving those around him the attention that used to come so easily. Now he just kept moving because it was the only alternative open to him.

One of his favourite maxims was, *When you can't move your body, move your mind; when you can't move your mind, move your body*. He had shared it with many of his clients and fans through his talks and writing. It had even formed a major part of one of his first books. He had never considered he would one day be so desperate, so close to breaking completely, he would apply it to himself.

Marcus was making his way to his office on High Pavement, a fashionable street on the edge of the Lace Market, one of Nottingham's trendiest areas. He had parked in the Victoria Centre car park nearly a mile away on the other side of the city. He was trying desperately to use the movement to get the voice and words of Peter Jones out of his mind.

Peter had met with him and Anne-Marie at their rented house in the valley. His best friend had, once again, turned into the terse, sharp-edged, professional Marcus had clashed with when Ethan first entered their lives. Only this time the DCI was even more direct, even more authoritative.

'You both need to be in a safe house. So let me do my job and get you out of here.'

'No.' Marcus hadn't even looked at his wife. 'We won last time and we'll win again. We've lost one home already.'

'This isn't a home. It's a bolthole. Last time you'd have died if you hadn't been lucky. And you've both got enough to manage without the increased stress of having to worry about Ethan.' Peter did look at Anne-Marie. She was staring out of the window.

'Last time you didn't know who you were looking for. This time you do.' Even though Marcus kept his gaze fixed on the detective, he'd seen Anne-Marie flinch at the word *bolthole*.

'Ethan might be unique, but he isn't a professional at this stuff. He can't evade you for long, can he?'

'It's not a question of how long he can stay free; it's a question of how much damage he can cause whilst he is. I'd have thought you'd have learnt by now, it doesn't take long to ruin or end a life.'

'If you follow that logic through, he can be caught in a minute too.'

'Would you get out of your arse!' Peter exploded. 'If you're not shit-scared, you bloody well should be! And if you are, there's no shame in admitting it! For Christ's sake, just make this as easy as possible for all of us! This is as real and as bad as it gets!'

Even with the terror coursing through his veins, Marcus couldn't help but look at the DCI and think of a volcano, powerful and still – immoveable – firing from its core. Only a fool would choose to hold his ground and attempt to divert what was heading his way, only a fool or someone incapable of moving. At that moment, Marcus reflected, he had probably been both. That was why he was making himself walk today. Better late than never.

Hopefully.

'We're not going anywhere,' he had said. 'We're not running away just because you can't do your job.'

'What?'

'You lost him. It seems to me that, having both been victims of Ethan, we're now both victims of police incompetence.'

'You're treading on very dangerous ground!'

Anne-Marie took a step closer to the window, her arms folded tightly across her chest.

'Why should stating the facts be dangerous?' Marcus retorted. 'I always thought that's what the police longed for.

Or is it that you only welcome facts when they support you?'

'You have no idea what you are talking about! The fact of the matter – the fact that matters above all else – is that I can only guarantee your safety if you do what I'm saying.'

'So you're admitting you can't protect us if we stay here, where we need to?'

The volcano shuddered briefly. 'I'm saying, as with all things in life, it makes sense to avoid unnecessary risk. Especially when your life is on the line!'

'Just because you managed to lose him, it doesn't follow that he'll come after me again. And even if he does, it doesn't follow that he'll come out on top. Last time he took me by surprise. He doesn't have that advantage anymore.'

'This is not a fucking sporting competition! And it isn't all about you and your overgrown ego!' Peter took a step back and forced himself to release his clenched fists. He offered his open palms as a sign of peace. 'Listen, please, if you can't do this for yourself, at least do it for Anne-Marie.'

For the first time both men looked at her. She shook her head silently, her eyes fixed, unblinking, on the view over the fields. 'Wherever you move us I'll take what's inside with me,' she said simply. 'And it won't stop you two fighting. Ethan Hall's a cancer. His presence in the world is corrosive. There's no location can change that.'

'So you want to stay here?' Peter's voice softened.

'Why not?' Anne-Marie's eyes watered. 'I think I need to be selfish.'

'Then I'll arrange a visit from a crime prevention officer. He'll sort out an alarm and offer some advice about personal security. It would be really good if you follow it.'

'Of course.' Anne-Marie forced a smile.

'If you both follow it.'

'Count me in.' Marcus's smile was a deliberate victory signal, intended to annoy. He had hoped that Peter Jones couldn't see past it.

20

'Wow, it's you!'

Marcus came out of his reverie and peered through the fog clouding his brain. At first the man in front of him was a dull grey shape, blocking his path, impossible to see beyond.

'You're Marcus Kline! What are the odds of that?'

'They're not exceptional. I've always been Marcus Kline.' The words were quick and aggressively defensive, just as they had been when addressing Peter. 'Who are you?'

'My name's Dave, Dave Johnson, I, er, unexpectedly found myself involved in your story a few months ago.'

'My story?' Marcus heard himself ask the unnecessary question and felt the colour draining from his face. The man had already given the game away, so why had he felt the need to double-check? The answer was simple: you double-check because when self-belief goes, the ability to trust your own skills and perception goes with it. Even if those skills and that level of perception have marked you out as one of the very best in the world.

I used to believe I was the best. Now a man who's obviously a reporter stops me and I still doubt myself.

'You're right. It's not just your story. It's the story of you and Ethan Hall.' Johnson spread his hands apologetically. 'Didn't mean to short-hand your experience.'

Marcus's vision was clearing in the heat of his anger. 'So, to go back to your original question, the odds were all stacked in your favour. You know where my office is and you're hanging around waiting to see me. The thing that really fucks me off is that you know who I am and what I do and you still decided you could get away with some bullshit 'who'd have thought it?' approach. So I'll tell you what Dave, let's call a spade a spade, you're a low-grade alcoholic reporter who's fucked up his life and is grabbing desperately at something that touched him somehow in some vague way, in the hope that if he's lucky he'll have his own thread bare story to tell the other early morning drinkers – in there and the other places where I'm sure you're much better known.'

Marcus was standing outside The Cross Keys pub. It was less than two hundred yards from his office. It was the place where Simon Westbury, his young and unbelievably enthusiastic protégé, used to breakfast most days of the week.

Used to.

Before Ethan Hall killed him in horrific fashion in what had been his final, perverse message to Marcus prior to his own terrifying confrontation.

Marcus forced himself to glance in the window as he spoke. The bar was empty. A young woman was cleaning tables, preparing for the day. She was about to clean the table where Simon used to sit. The acid in Marcus's stomach burnt as she went about her work. He turned his attention back to the reporter. Johnson was heavily overweight, with sallow skin and patches of darkness beneath his eyes.

'I'll tell you what I'll do Dave, because I never want it to be said that I don't support and help journalists in their noble search for the truth.' Marcus noticed that his toes were flexing and gripping the earth as he spoke. The anger was acting as a release, helping him to reconnect with the planet and the air and the people around him. He was back, if only for a moment, to being the Marcus Kline who could really listen and really see and who could, consequently, influence others with apparent ease. The words came, precise, paced and sequenced to create a very deliberate outcome. Dave Johnson, on the receiving end, found himself thinking later of a professional boxer striking in combination with irresistible speed and accuracy.

'I never want you to think that I would stand in your way of a good story. After all, we all have our job to do and, if it's in the public interest, they deserve to know, don't they? They deserve to know your interpretation of serious, serious, events in people's lives – of threatening, life changing, even life ending events – that you frame and diminish beneath trashy headlines, shred down into column inches, and turn into gutter trash. So, here's the thing. I'm going to give you an exclusive – an exclusive chance to ask me one question. Anything you want! How about that? And, to make things even better, I acknowledge right now that both your question and my answer are on the record. How does that sound, Dave?'

Johnson took an involuntary step back as the intended double hit of surprise and fear rocked him. To Marcus's amazement he regrouped quickly, forcing himself to nod with clearly feigned confidence as he regained the lost ground.

'C'mon Dave, you've got one shot! Make it your best!' Marcus fired the words out, fascinated to see their effect. This time the heavy man absorbed them without flinching. Despite himself, Marcus couldn't help but think *Good for you!* For a fraction of a second he imagined himself stepping forwards to confront Ethan Hall again. He hoped he'd have the same courage. He hoped his fear wouldn't be so obvious.

'Right,' the journalist glanced upwards and to his right as he searched to construct the best possible question. Marcus watched and gave him time. What he'd started as an attack was turning into something else. Johnson didn't give him time to decide what. 'Here's the question I want to ask you. And I want you to be completely honest.'

'Go on.'

'Right,' Johnson said again. He coughed, covering his mouth briefly with his hand. 'My question is, what have you learnt about yourself since you've been targeted by Ethan Hall?'

Many years before, Marcus had sat in a ringside seat watching Kirkland Laing, the greatest boxer ever to come from Nottingham, in his last fight. It had been on his home turf at the Victoria Baths in Sneinton, a small and insignificant venue for a man who, in his day, had been arguably the best pound for pound boxer in the world. Despite overwhelming his opponent in the early rounds, Laing went on to lose to a young man who wouldn't have laid a glove on him in his prime. When asked to explain it, Marcus heard Laing's trainer Mickey Duff say simply with a shrug of his shoulders, 'Old Father Time...'

Now, as Johnson's question thudded into his psyche, more powerful and penetrative than he had expected, Marcus couldn't help but remember the look on the ageing boxer's face as he realised, finally, there was no turning back.

'What have I learnt?' Marcus stalled, buying himself a few precious seconds as he tried desperately to organise his internal processing.

'Yes. Precisely that.'

It was Marcus' turn to nod. A tumble of images, emotions and thoughts rolled through him. He saw Anne-Marie standing in the kitchen of their old house, their home, looking out at the willow tree, knowing she had cancer, keeping her secret from him and everyone else. He saw Simon and Emma, his former PA and receptionist, standing face-to-face in his office enjoying one of their many pretend arguments, their eyes sparkling with affection. He saw Emma's tear-stained face on the day she left, needing to escape the workplace that had once been filled with understanding and learning and fun, and now held too many painful associations. He saw the scalpel in Ethan Hall's hand as he prepared to make the first cut. He saw Ethan's eyes, unblinking, filled with a certainty of unfathomable depth. He felt the tape holding him in place, keeping him prisoner, making him helpless. He felt the pressure squeezing him again and found himself falling into the emptiness inside where his own certainty had once been.

His mind began to fog.

He fought it by grasping for the anger that had cleansed him only a few minutes before. He stamped his right foot. He shook his head. Felt a jolt of something close to rage fire up his spine. He thought of all the reasons why Ethan Hall deserved to be captured and locked away forever. He forced his imagination to picture Simon Westbury's violent, needless death. He felt another jolt, more powerful this time. He watched the fog dissolve as his emotion spread. He realised that, for the first time in his life, he genuinely hated another human being.

The reporter was suddenly there again, obvious to him in every detail. As obvious as the learning this encounter had unexpectedly provided. Marcus felt a smile spread across his face. He knew now what he going to say; knew with absolute clarity what he wanted to achieve. The reporter's question was not the intrusive challenge it was meant to be. It was a glorious opportunity. One he simply couldn't – and shouldn't – resist.

'Dave, I'm going to tell you everything I've learnt about myself because of these terrible and tragic events, I'm going to share with you just what it means to be me right now.'

Johnson couldn't even come close to keeping the surprise off his face.

Marcus let his smile broaden and the words pour out.

He was going on the attack.

21

Anne-Marie needed to talk. She needed to talk to someone who could listen to, understand and protect what she had to say. Furthermore, that person had to be able to resist her emotional angst. They had to be trustworthy, caring and somewhat detached all at the same time. In Anne-Marie's mind there was only one choice.

Yet still she hesitated. She had picked up her mobile phone twice, brought up the person's number, looked at it, then replaced the phone on the kitchen table without making the call. She had wasted a couple of hours battling what she had come to realise was fear.

How ridiculous was that? Scared of making a phone call. Scared of talking. Scared of saying what needed to be said with someone she knew she could trust. It was just one more of the many things cancer did to you the doctors never warned you about.

Anne-Marie picked up the phone again. The fear urged her to open her new emails instead of making the call. She won the battle and pressed the image of the green phone before she had time to falter.

Third time lucky.

Unless the call rang through. And if it did she couldn't be sure when – or if – she would find the strength to do this again. Or if she would even be able leave a voice message.

The silence before the connection was made seemed to last forever. A memory filled the space. A memory of the last time she had called this number. Then, as now, her hands were shaking.

The phone started ringing. The fear fed on the noise just as it had the silence. The question stabbed like a surgeon's knife.

How many rings before it cuts to answerphone? At some point in the last few months it had become instinctive to measure and count everything. To reduce life down to the most basic and precious commodity: Time.

How many more days before the season changes?

How much longer can I keep going like this?

How many breaths before I die?

Anne-Marie pressed the phone tight against her ear. She couldn't resist the urge to count the rings. Two...three...four... five...Not many more before the answerphone kicked in, surely? Six...seven...eight...*For God's sake, speak to me!* The silent plea was as frequent as – and often stimulated by – the silent counting. *Please! I don't know if I can do this again!* Nine... ten...

'Anne-Marie.'

The voice offered no obvious welcome, no happy-to-hear-from-you implication, no curious, questioning tone. Instead just a terse, strong sense of impatience, urgency and power forcing out the syllables.

'Yes!' It was the voice she needed to hear; different from every other time she had heard him speak apart from that unforgettable night when she had called, terrified and shaking. It was a voice and a moment she had replayed many times in her dreams. His certainty, authority and control had been as reassuring as it was surprising.

'You only do what I tell you! Do anything else and you will get yourself and Marcus killed! Do you understand?'

That night she had understood. She had done as she was told. Marcus had been saved. Now she needed that same version of him again; the version she hadn't known existed until the worst of times.

'Peter! Thank you!' Anne-Marie gasped, drawing back what could so easily have turned into a sob. She was sure he must have heard it, although he gave nothing in response. She spoke quickly into the silence. 'I'm sorry for calling you. It's just that I need to talk to someone and if I don't I know I'm going to explode or implode or something. I just have to get this out and even though Marcus is Marcus – actually because Marcus is Marcus – I can't do this with him and I don't have anyone else to turn to who can do what, *be* what, I need right now. So I had to call you. And I tried not to. I really, really tried. Only even though I was scared I just didn't have a choice. And I can't even begin to imagine what things must be like for you, but I knew that if I didn't …'

'– Anne-Marie.' He used her name to stop her.

'Yes?'

'What is it you need to get out?' He laid the question down like a stepping-stone.

She took it, desperate for release, aware there was no turning back. 'I'm dying,' she said. It was the first time she had said it out loud. 'I'm not a cancer sufferer. I'm not managing a serious illness. I'm not just a series of numbers pulled from medical assessments. I'm dying! And there's nothing anyone can do about it!'

'Is that what you know or what you believe?'

'It's what I feel inside, more than I've ever felt anything. More even than…' For a second the memory of a moon reflecting on a dark Asian sea took her attention. Then the pressure of the moment reasserted itself. She had to say this now or it would become just one more thing growing unwelcome inside her. '… That night, when I saw Ethan Hall had taken Marcus prisoner, when I called you panic stricken, that night was the only time I've totally forgotten about my cancer. Can you imagine that?

It took a madman with a knife to make me forget. And even then it was only for a few hours. Apart from that, it's always been there, even when I'm not consciously aware of it. It's like a shadow in my mind, a shadow with life and weight, silently drawing my energy. So, yes, I can say – need to say – that I'm dying. And if I took a photograph of myself right now, that's what the title would be, it's what the story would be about.'

'If you did a self-portrait right now and called it *Dying*, I'd think you'd got the title wrong.' His voice was so matter-of-fact he could have been discussing the correct way to reference a part of something complex like an engine.

Anne-Marie pressed her right hand against the kitchen table for support. He waited for her to ask. 'What would you call it?'

'I'd call it *Processing*. I think that would be the most honest and powerful descriptor.' Once again he gave her time, but not enough for her to work out what she wanted to say next. 'Now,' he said, 'I have to go and do some processing of my own. Remember, though, you can call me anytime you need to. I'm always here.'

'Thank you.' She felt the hesitation again and pushed through it quickly. 'Peter, just one more thing?'

'Yes.'

'You won't tell anyone about this conversation, will you?'

'You have my word.' He hung up without saying goodbye. She couldn't help but wonder if that was because he was so busy, or because he was making a point.

22

Calvin Brent was never too busy to make a point. His reputation and authority depended upon it. He knew, too, from more than a decade of playing poker at the highest level, that the value of the cards in your hand was only determined by when and how you played them. Ethan Hall was a card of rare significance and rare threat. The first quality meant he had to be used to achieve a most important advantage; the second that he had to be used and disposed of swiftly. Calvin had his plan in place.

At the poker table if you wanted to make the most of your power cards, you had to be capable of bluff and double bluff. You also had to be willing to risk or even sacrifice some cards of lesser value. Calvin sat behind his desk and looked up at Matt. The enforcer was trying hard not to fidget. It was, Calvin thought, as if Ethan Hall's influence had damaged his internal wiring. Whether the damage was permanent or not, Calvin had neither the time nor the desire to find out. In the final analysis, cards were just cards. You picked them up, you changed them, you put them down; you started again with a new pack. Cards were just a means to an end.

'Tell me,' Calvin said, 'are you clear about what you have to do?'

'Absolutely, boss. I've got it down. Bang on!' Matt fidgeted some more, his eyes flickering from side to side.

'So tell me what you have to do this morning.' Brent leant forwards across his desk. 'Every detail.'

'I pick Hall up at the agreed place, then I drive him to the target. I stay outside 'till he's finished, then I go and check. Then I call and let you know.'

'And then?'

'I tell 'im you want us to pick a package up so we 'ave to take a detour on our way to 'is first target.'

'And?'

'When we get to the warehouse I'll tell 'im to come inside with me and you think 'e'll say 'No' because 'e'll be suspicious. Then I'll try to persuade 'im.'

'What happens next?'

'I don't know boss.'

'Why not?'

'You 'aven't told me.' The big man looked up at the ceiling.

'That's right. Do you know why I haven't told you?'

'No boss.'

'Of course you do. It's for your own safety. Ethan Hall has already messed with your head. The less I put in there, the less he can get out. Once he realises you don't know anything, he won't do anything to you. Do you understand?'

Matt nodded.

'Good. You're important to me, Matt. I've got plans for you. You just get Ethan to where I need him to be after he's done the first job, I'll take care of the rest. Ethan Hall will soon be out of your head forever. I promise.'

'Thank you boss.'

Calvin eased back in his chair and smiled reassuringly. The generally accepted wisdom was that the best lie contained a good deal of truth. The lesser-known wisdom, the sort understood only by him and those rare few others who had achieved great power, was that the most important truths contained the worst of all possible outcomes wrapped in easy-to-get-hold-of hope.

Before the end of the day Ethan Hall would be dead and his body disappeared. And to make sure the odds were stacked even more in his favour, Calvin had also arranged for Matt to experience the same fate.

Even low-value cards, he mused, have their role to play. And if played well, which often meant sacrificing them, they could contribute significantly to the overall result.

'You don't have to thank me,' Calvin said. 'You're an important part of my winning hand, Matt. And you can be absolutely sure I'll play it to perfection. After all, that's what I do.'

23

Influence the Marcus Kline Consultancy was based on the south side of High Pavement in a grade II listed building that dated back to the late eighteenth century. Marcus Kline used to think of his office as his most personal of all playgrounds. Not anymore. Not since the life had been driven out of it.

Emma's departure had hurt him, but it hadn't come as a shock. Fight-flight-or freeze; the three primal alternatives. Flight was the most common and usually the most sensible choice. No surprise then that Emma had simply followed her gut instinct and moved away.

He didn't know where. She had said she was going to travel, see things, go to places, hoping that difference would act as a cleanser. She had promised she would call once she felt safe enough again to stop moving. He was still waiting.

Emma had been the nearest thing he had ever had to a daughter. Not that he had ever told her. Not that he had told anyone.

Some things are better left unsaid.

The irony of that thought forced the sort of painful smile he imagined all parents felt sooner or later.

Marcus was standing in the silence of his reception, his left hand resting on the desk that used to be Emma's. He had made no attempt to replace her yet. He hadn't replaced Simon either. He couldn't. This wasn't his playground anymore. It was just an empty space.

Filled with shadow-pain.

Marcus flinched and looked round the room; heard nothing but his thoughts.

Shadow-pain.

That was the source of his mind fog, the reason why his self-belief was ebbing away. Shadow-pain. You couldn't run away from it. You had to stand and fight. Step into it. Go on the attack.

'I was right to give Johnson a story,' he said out loud. 'Ethan doesn't expect me to come back fighting. And just because I lost once doesn't mean anything. I'm right to be angry, to use it as my strength. It will make the difference this time.'

Marcus removed his hand from Emma's desk and walked through into his own office. His mobile phone rang. He didn't recognise the number. He stared at it, feeling the phone buzz in his hand. It was, he realised, the first chance he'd had to talk to someone from this place for several months, since Emma had gone, since he had stopped being available for clients, since he had started hiding away, camouflaging his fear behind the need to write *Belief*. It was an unexpected and frightening opportunity to act as the great consultant again.

I can't run away from it.

The phone stopped ringing. He kept hold, kept watching in case a voice message had been left. He waited longer than he needed to. There was nothing. No potential new client. Not even an old friend just touching base. Maybe it had been a wrong number? After all, he wasn't the centre of the universe anymore. He was more a damaged spacecraft in danger of spinning out of control than a powerful star. He considered briefly flicking through his list of contacts and calling one of them at random.

Hi. Yes, it's me. I'm just calling to say...

To say what?

To say what, actually?

I'm just calling to pass the time of day. Well, actually, I'm calling so that I can practise talking to people whilst I'm in my office.

Marcus closed his fist around the phone, squeezing momentarily before dropping it onto his desk. He still couldn't take his eyes off it. For some reason it made him think of a large black-cased insect, confident in its body armour. The temptation to smash it thudded through his veins.

And then someone knocked on the door. Three times, with urgency.

24

Ethan Hall closed the passenger door and settled into the black, leather seat of the Mercedes as if he owned both the car and the driver. Matt stared straight ahead, his hands gripping the steering wheel.

'Let's go play,' Ethan said. He waited until the car had pulled away and joined the line of traffic, moving slowly towards the city centre before adding, 'Why don't I have the list of addresses?'

'Boss's orders.' Matt's focus was fixed firmly on the car in front.

'You have the list, right?'

'Nope.'

'So how do you know where to take me?'

'I'm gonna ring for instructions after you've done the first job.' Matt blinked.

'Aah, I see. Your boss has a plan.

'Dunno. Nothing t'do with me.'

'Everything is to do with everybody. One way or another.'

'Don't know nothin' about that.'

'You'll learn.' As the car came to a temporary halt Ethan made a point of easing his head back against the headrest and closing his eyes. In the darkness he could feel even more clearly the big man's heart hammering in his chest. He sighed gently, enjoying the contrast, enjoying the sublime pleasure of waiting for the inevitable. It proved, as expected, to be a brief wait.

' 'Ow d'ya do it?'

'Do what?' Ethan kept his eyes closed.

'Make people do things.'

'We all make people do things.'

'I mean the way you make people do things…the things you make people do.'

'I look at them and I hear what's going on inside. I listen to them and I see their thoughts and their feelings.'

'That don't make sense.'

'Want me to prove it – again? Want me to open my eyes and show you?'

'You won't do that.'

'I've got to open my eyes sometime.'

'I mean you won't do … do owt t'me.'

'Why do you think that?'

'Because I'm driving.'

'You'll stop when we get to where we're going.'

'Yeah, but you'll still need me.'

'To do what?'

'Take you to the other places.'

'You don't know the other places. You've just told me that.'

'But I will know once I report back. And besides, I'm the boss's eyes and ears.'

'I'll tell him you said that.'

'You won't get t'speak to 'im again.' Matt flushed. Ethan felt it.

'Is that a fact?'

'Yeah.'

Ethan lapsed into silence, enjoying the changes he was creating in the other man's heartbeat. In another life, he mused, he might have been the world's greatest conductor. 'I see them as colours,' he said.

'What?'

'Your feelings. The responses you try to keep secret. I see them as colours in the air around you. I see how my expressions and gestures and words affect you, how your colours change when I influence you.'

'That ain't right.'

'Is it not?'

'No. I mean, I'm not saying yo'r lyin' or anythin'. Or that yo'r mad in the 'ead.'

'Good.'

'It's just that, y'know, I've never 'eard of anyone who can do stuff like that. So if yo'r the only one it ain't, y'know, normal.'

'Did it feel normal having a gun in your mouth, feeling your finger pressing the trigger, feeling your tongue on the metal?'

Matt licked his lips, loud as a wave lapping on a beach. 'You don't 'ave t' be a cunt.'

'You didn't have to take it like a cunt.'

'I... I didn' 'ave a choice.'

'That's right. But you're used to that. You and all the rest. That's what being normal means. Just doing what someone else makes you do. And those people who make you do things are nowhere near as talented as me. They're not special. They are just loud. And ballsy. And so full of themselves they don't realise how pathetic they are.' Ethan sniffed. 'You know I can do anything I want with you?'

The car pulled to a halt. 'We're 'ere.' Matt switched the engine off and shifted in his seat. 'It's time fer you t'do wha' we came for.'

Ethan Hall opened his eyes. Matt was staring deliberately out of the driver's door window. It reminded Ethan of a time many years before when, late at night, a young, drunk reveller had pushed into the back of a city taxi ahead of him, and how the driver had deliberately looked away and then covered his ears as Ethan punished the man.

It's what the herd does – pretends by looking at nothing.

'You're going to stay here and look as if you're watching the traffic.'

'Yeah. 'Ow did y'know?'

'Because I'm not normal.'

'I'll come in when yo'r done. Just t'check.'

'Boss's orders?'

'Yeah. And ya need t'get it right.'

'That's brave.' Ethan chuckled. 'Your Boss doesn't have to worry. It'll be natural.'

Ethan got out of the Mercedes and looked at the building for the first time. An involuntary smile crossed his face. He stepped forward without hesitation and knocked on the door. Three times, with urgency.

25

Marcus Kline opened the door and took a pace back automatically. He couldn't help but swallow as the adrenaline surged through his system. There had been a time – it was most of his life – when he could never be taken by surprise. That had been the time before Ethan Hall. That time seemed an age away; memories and ways of being that were now in danger of fragmenting and dissolving forever in the heat of the present.

Fight!

Marcus forced himself to hold his ground. He looked deliberately over the shoulders of the person stepping into his doorway. It was where he always looked when working at his best, when wanting to see and hear with the clarity that produced great insight. It had been one of his first great discoveries, one of the most important weapons in his communication arsenal. He needed it now.

Marcus looked into the space behind and around the person's head, softening his gaze, resisting the temptation to focus on details, letting his peripheral vision dominate, trusting it to show him what he most needed to see.

He saw absolute commitment. And desperation.

Understanding piggybacked his adrenaline. Thoughts of self disappeared. He felt the words, unknown, as yet lacking completeness, forming deep in his belly. He said the name first, using it as a gateway and an invitation.

'Diane.'

'Mr Kline! Oh, I'm so pleased you're here! I've tried several times in the last few months and I was beginning to think you'd closed down or gone away or something. And then I saw in the papers about that awful thing with Ethan Hall escaping and that made everything even worse and I thought I'll try just one more time, but he's really not going to be there now. And I was wrong! And you are – and you even remembered me!' The woman's eyes watered. She dabbed the tears away with the un-self-conscious ease of a person used to crying.

'Diane, come inside.' Marcus stepped to his right, gesturing into the space of the reception with his open left hand. She followed as if on a lead. He closed the door behind her and, as he looked into her eyes, he smiled gently. She couldn't help but return it. Her cheeks were flushed. She ignored the moisture on them.

He had met Diane Clusker only once before, by accident when she had been shopping with her husband, Paul. They almost bumped into each other outside the Theatre Royal. Paul had been one of the regular low-fee clients he worked with as a way of giving something back to his local community. Paul had contacted him asking for help to improve his business communications. What he had also needed – and didn't know how to ask for – was a way of diminishing the negative influences of his past. In Marcus' experience, every expressed request for help was a psychological form of Trojan horse, carrying hidden within it the person's secret need and agenda. It had been easy for Marcus to create the changes Paul required. Easy and pointless. The memory of their last meeting flittered in front of his mind's eye, making his scalp crawl.

'What can I do for you, Diane?' He asked quickly, grateful for the protection of the words and the way they shifted him from his head to his stomach.

'I need you to help me. The way you were helping Paul. The way you were changing his relationship with the past. I can't deal with anything anymore. It all keeps pulling me back.

It's like a bad dream. You know the sort I mean, it's a dream in which you try to get away from something terrible and, no matter what you do, you just can't. And since that…that man… has been allowed to get free, it's got so much worse.' Her tears flowed. 'How can they have been so stupid? I mean, they had him and then…then…It's like it's all around me now. Before it was just inside me, just my memories and all the connections and the reminders, but now that he's out it's on the inside and the outside. I've got nowhere to go but here, to you.'

'I understand. Let's move somewhere else.' Marcus cupped Diane's left elbow with his right hand and steered her into his office.

We both need to keep moving.

Paul Clusker had been Ethan Hall's second victim. At least, the second the police were aware of. He had been killed in his own home. He had been chosen because of his connection to Marcus. And Marcus couldn't help but blame himself. As he did for the other deaths, as he did for the way Ethan was destroying the lives of those he hadn't killed.

'How are you coping?' Diane asked suddenly. 'I'm so sorry, I should have asked sooner. After all, I'm sure it's…Well, it must be awful for you, too.'

'I'm more concerned for you, right now. You are my…'

Defence mechanism.

'…priority. You were right to be persistent. Otherwise you wouldn't be here now and I wouldn't be helping you. Isn't that true?'

'Yes. Yes, it is.'

'That's right. You are right. To be. Hear.' Marcus felt himself ease towards the edges of the hypnotic state he was leading

Diane into. He would hold himself there as Diane went ever deeper. He couldn't help but notice just how much of a release it felt for him, too. "You are right because that important part, deep inside, the part that is beyond your conscious awareness even as you find yourself going deeper now trying to find it, that part is truly more resource-full than we can ever imagine. And you can believe in it, can you not, because it just feels right. Hear. Now. Isn't it? Please, sit down. All the way down.' Marcus pulled the chair back, away from his desk. Diane Clusker sat without hesitation. Her eyes closed instantly.

26

Ethan Hall felt his eyes widen. He felt his pupils dilate. He knew he was seeing the other man with a clarity no one else on Earth could imagine. He watched the colours of surprise and uncertainty flickering out and around him. He waited, watching and learning. Thrilled.

'Yes? How can I help you?' The man asked.

'Don't you remember me?' Ethan breathed the words across the space between them. 'Don't you. Remember.'

The man blinked as he tried to follow the command and found himself struggling to access an appropriate memory. Ethan gave him four seconds, letting the silence and his stillness add weight to the pressure.

'Aren't you going to invite me in?' He said.

'Yes. Yes, of course.' The man stepped to one side. 'Please.'

Ethan walked through the hall and into the lounge as if he had been there many times before. He heard the door close. He felt the man's confusion as he followed him into the room. It was like snow, swirling in a breeze. It made Ethan's skin tingle.

'Robin,' he said, 'how could you forget me?'

'I really don't know. I'm so sorry. I'm usually so good at this sort of thing.'

'Of course you are. Let me remind you. We met at that party. We talked about your allergy. Or rather, you did. You spent quite some time telling me about the terrible reaction you suffer when eating nuts, how you were one of those unfortunate few individuals for whom it's actually life threatening. Don't you remember?'

'Er, no. No, I'm sorry.' Robin frowned.

'Don't worry. It will come to you. I'm sure of that. We both know it's important to always remember an allergy when it's so serious. So you will remember our chat. You will remember how I explained to you that some researchers in immunology and genetics consider allergies to be like a phobia of the immune system. By which they mean that an allergy is a result of something happening neurologically and not just physiologically. Which means, of course, that an allergy – even one like yours – is open to influence.

'I told you, for example, of some people whose allergic symptoms would disappear if they were distracted or fell asleep whilst experiencing a reaction. Isn't that amazing! One second they are in the midst of a most terrible allergic reaction and the next they are OK! Tell me, Robin, can you imagine that happening to you? Thinking now about how your body responds so severely to any interaction with nuts, can you imagine the symptoms just vanishing? Go on, thinking about it, try. Now.'

Ethan gestured towards the settee. Robin sat down abruptly. Ethan remained standing, watching the first signs of changes in the other man's pallor, the first subtle shift in his breathing.

'No,' Robin said. 'I can't imagine anything like that. I can only think of how…how horrible it is…how scared I become.'

'You can't imagine it Robin, because you don't believe strongly enough, because you've allowed yourself to become limited. Locked in. You're malfunctioning, just like your immune system now. You see, your allergic reaction is a result of your immune system overreacting. Let me tell you precisely how this is happening now. You do want to keep listening, don't you?'

Robin nodded. There was an obvious redness on his cheeks and throat.

'Of course. And you are right to. Just trust the feeling, Robin.' Ethan ran his left hand briefly across his face and then continued. 'Your immune system is made up of different cells all with different functions. The macrophage is like a scavenger cell. Its job is to capture and ingest any foreign substances that might get into the body – things like grass or hay or, in your case, nuts. The great thing about the macrophage cell is that it doesn't ingest the entire virus; it also alerts the rest of the immune system to the current invasion by displaying a part of it. This gets the attention of the helper T cells. Their job is to determine whether or not the invaders are dangerous. They do this by connecting themselves to the part of the invader being displayed. If there is a match, these helper T cells send out an urgent message for help to the killer T cells. What happens next is all because of these killers, Robin. Can you feel it?'

Robin nodded again. The redness was darkening and spreading. His breathing was faster, more laboured. He was staring into space, seemingly unaware of Ethan. The synesthete shivered with excitement.

'I've spent several months in a coma,' he said. 'It's a very special place to be. Trust me. The only downside is that you don't get to enter into the lives of others; you don't get to influence. I didn't realise at first how much I missed it. Anyway, let's get back to those killers. They are fighters. They rush to where the intruder is being flagged. They inject it with a chemical and explode it. Bang! Internal explosions! Imagine that. It's a battlefield inside your own body, Robin. And it's a good and appropriate battle if it's a virus or form of bacteria being blown up. The problem occurs – your problem occurs – when these killers attack healthy cells. Which is precisely what happens every time you have an allergic reaction, Robin. Your immune system has got its coding wrong where nuts are concerned. So it goes on the attack. Exploding cells it doesn't actually need to. And one of the chemicals released – no, let's be more precise, here, one of the chemicals excreted – when the cells explode is histamine. You know that one, don't you Robin? You know how makes you feel?'

'Yeth.'

'Of course, you do. In fact, it looks to me that your mouth and lips are tingling already. Isn't that so?'

'Yeth.'

'And your face is starting to swell and when it feels like this, if you don't take your tablet immediately it will just keep on swelling. Isn't that right?'

'Yeth.'

'Only you can't move, can you, because you can't feel your legs or your feet. Isn't that right.'

'Mmm.'

'You can only feel your face swelling and your lips and mouth tingling and your throat swelling too and the sickness in your stomach.'

'Mmm.'

'And the only thing you can notice and respond to, apart from all of these feelings, is the sound of my voice. And a thing you might not know, and you need to know it because it's happening inside you now, is that the release of histamine also creates constriction in the lungs. Which is why you are finding it more and more difficult to breathe, which is why you are starting to wheeze, and it's right and proper that you do, because life is worth fighting for even though you know deep in your unconscious, listening to me now, that it's a useless fight. It's a fight you can't win as everything reddens and swells and constricts with every word I say, with every sentence I breathe into you, creating explosions within an increasingly confined space. Battlefields become crammed, Robin, debris blocks every way in and out. Blink if you feel it.'

Robin blinked.

'Good boy. And I can hear how your precious heart is going so fast now. It's telling you how desperate it's getting, how it can't do anything apart from to keep going faster and faster until you have to lose consciousness. Blink, Robin, if you can feel and hear its fear.'

Robin blinked.

'It's called anaphylaxis, but I'm sure you know that. Anaphylaxis. It's the worst kind of allergic reaction; it's the one you dread. It's the killer, Robin. Making your skin get redder and redder, and the rashes spreading, and your face and throat swelling and swelling, and your lips and mouth tingling uncontrollably as the feeling of sickness stresses your gut even more, pressing, trying to burst out, and you can hear the wheezing and even, though you know it's you doing it, it seems somehow distant as your heart pounds and pounds and races and screams for it all to stop, and now – incredibly, amazingly – you feel your blood pressure dropping away and unconsciousness rushes just as your stomach does.'

Robin vomited. He swallowed, gagged, and coughed dark red fluid and chunks of thick brown matter on to his chin. He didn't notice. His eyes began to glaze.

'Ooo, Robin, it even looks like bits of nut coming out for a final farewell.' Ethan applauded briefly. 'Walnut, I would say, although it is hard to be certain, even for someone like me. You don't just have to make your mouth do all the work, though. It is a battlefield, remember, desperate times call for desperate measures. Seek escape every way you can.'

Robin lost control of his bowels.

'Wow! Big effort! Doesn't it take you right back to being an infant again?' Ethan straightened. 'Only Mummy's not here. And there's no ambulance, either. No blee-blaa, blee-blaa sounds coming your way, Robin. Just your heart screaming and your skin bursting and your throat pulling inwards on itself. And unconsciousness…unconsciousness, Robin, the only way out, as inevitable as me clapping my hands. Now!'

Robin eyes rolled into the back of his head. He released a deep, guttural sigh and his body slumped. His head dropped forwards. The sudden silence emphasised the loss. Ethan Hall was reminded of the stink in Darren's house. When he opened the front door and signalled for Matt to come in, he took a moment to breathe in the fresh air.

27

'Christ! It's like a shithouse!' Matt spun on his heels as if he was going to exit the room.

'What do you think an abattoir smells like?' Ethan made a point of keeping his face expressionless.

The big man turned back and looked again at the body. 'What the fuck did you to 'im?'

'We had a chat. His body didn't like it.'

'Yo're fuckin' tellin' me it didn't.' Matt squinted. ''E's dead, right?'

'You'll need to check.'

'I'm not touchin' that!'

'Then how will you be sure? And you do need to be sure when you talk to your boss, don't you?'

'Jesus Christ!' Matt turned and took a step towards the body. 'Couldn't you 'ave killed 'im and left 'is insides in?'

'Life always goes from the inside out. Haven't you noticed that? That's the inevitable journey.'

'I 'ave no fuckin' idea what yo'r talkin' abowt.' Matt looked at the settee and pulled a face. 'I'm not sitting on that.'

'Then squat. That would be the most appropriate thing to do anyway. Just squat and check his pulse.'

Matt squatted. Ethan watched him reach out gingerly with his right hand and press his forefinger against Robin's carotid artery. He loved the hesitation and the obvious distaste. He could barely wait for the next part. It didn't take long.

'What the fuck?' Matt pulled his finger away and cocked his head, trying to look more closely at Robin's face. He scowled, gave up, and pushed two fingers more forcefully against his throat. 'Shit!' He straightened and glared at Ethan. ''E's still fuckin' breathin'!'

'Nothing escapes you, does it?'

'Shit! Shit!' Matt stamped the floor. 'You were s'posed t'kill 'im! That was yo'r fuckin' job! That was the deal!'

'That was the deal that suited your boss. It wasn't the deal that suited me. The deal that suits me is the one that gets me to visit the people I need to and keeps my plan on track.'

'Fuck yo'r plans! What the fuck am I s'posed t'do now?'

'Call your boss, just as he told you to. Tell him what has happened.'

'What 'as 'appened?'

'Robin's in a coma. If he doesn't receive any medical attention – and you told me he's a very solitary guy – he'll most probably die in that coma sometime in the next forty-eight hours. However, if your boss does what I want that's a gamble you don't need to take, because once you've driven me to see everyone on my list, we'll come back here and, if necessary, I'll have another word or two in his ear and he will stop breathing once and for all. It's as simple as that. So, you want to know what's happened, Matt? I'll tell you. I've fucking happened. And right now Robin is my…'

Protection

'…message and guarantee.'

'Yo'r a fuckin'…'

'Stop searching for words you don't know and make the call.'

Matt took out his phone. His hand was shaking. Ethan couldn't stop himself from saying, 'When you are under pressure and you can't fight, flee or freeze it all just rattles around inside you. Don't worry, though, I won't put you into a coma. As long as you're a good boy.'

Matt stared at the carpet until his call was answered. It was clear from the beginning he was struggling to keep to the agreed script. 'I delivered the present t'the right address.' Pause. 'No, It wasn't received as fully as expected.' Pause. 'It's nearly as good as y'wanted, just not over the line yet.' Pause. 'After the other visits.'

Ethan clicked his fingers. 'Give me the phone. Tell him I understand the rules.'

'The present-maker wants a word.' Pause. 'He knows that.' Pause. 'Yes, boss.' Matt handed over the mobile.

Ethan spoke first. 'All is well and under control. We are on our way to making everyone happy. The first receiver hasn't fully opened his present. However he's definitely in the right state of mind to wait until I return to finish it off. Which is what needs to happen. We need to change the delivery completion sequence, reschedule things so that I come back here as soon as I've delivered the other gifts to my satisfaction. That's the only way we – you – can please all involved.'

Calvin Brent snorted. 'There's always more than one way.'

'Indeed. It's just that some ways involve more risk and less certainty. And when there's no need to choose one of those ways why would you? It's all a matter of timing, isn't it? As long as everything gets done, what difference does it make? Especially when the alternative is really very, very unhelpful.'

'We can all be unhelpful.'

'To varying degrees. My point is this is only a minor change; you just need to let my taxi know where to go next. Then we are back on schedule, just in a different order.'

'And what if I don't?'

'That's easy. The worst-case scenario is that no one then gets the present they desire. The best-case scenario is that only one of us does.'

'The question is, if that happens, which one of us ends up

the happiest?'

'The one who doesn't feel like he's got a gun in his mouth, metaphorically speaking. And when there's no need to feel like that, why would you?' Ethan breathed softly into the phone. 'It's always best to take the easiest way out, isn't it?'

'I find it's always best to do the things that make me most happy. I find that when I'm happy most other people are, too.'

'Most people – not everyone?'

'You can't please all of the people all of the time.'

'So true. That's why we're having to change the schedule.'

'How so?'

'I'm concerned that if we stick to the original schedule I won't be in the *most* category. In fact, I'm certain your original schedule will guarantee that I'm not. And for our agreement to work we have to re-organise it to ensure our mutual satisfaction.'

'I think you're being unnecessarily cautious. I think you're seeing problems where non exist.'

Ethan laughed. 'I don't need to see problems to recognise them. That's a very mundane way of going about things. No, I hear problems. I hear them on the breath. I hear them being formed. I hear their structure and timing. And I smell their purpose.'

'I think you talk shit.'

'No you don't. Although not too many minutes ago I was talking shit in a manner of speaking.'

'What?'

'Private joke. Between me and my driver.' Ethan glanced at Matt. 'Anyway, it's time to make a decision. Are you going to ignore the odds and push your luck, like an amateur who treats life as if it's a lottery, or will you bide your time and play the cards you've just been dealt?'

'I'm the boss. I decide the options open to me.'

'Of course you do.'

The sarcasm was treacle thick. Calvin Brent pulled the phone away from his ear and glared at it, his mind filling with the image of Ethan Hall's arrogant face dead, with holes where the eyes used to be and the tongue ripped out.

'It will never happen.'

Ethan's words leapt out from the phone, demanding a response. Calvin spoke before he could think of alternatives. 'You listen to me you freak! You need to understand that everything I want to make happen happens! This is my world. So whatever you think you're talking about really doesn't matter a toss.'

'I was talking about those thoughts that were just filling your mind. How vivid and impossible they were. I was talking about how you need to keep your eyes open to new alternatives.'

Calvin swallowed. 'I know alternatives you can't even imagine.'

'Breathing gives everyone away. Trust me. It's the best of all presents. Which is why it's time to agree our new schedule and move on. Tick-tock. Tick-tock.'

'The clock's ticking for you, too. Remember that.'

'It's something I'm counting on. Now, so you can cling on to your pretence of power, why don't we let you make your decisions one at a time? The first thing you have to decide is that you are going to give Matt the addresses of the people I need to talk to.'

Calvin tried desperately to clear his mind, to identify the strategy that would put him back in control of the game. His thoughts, though, kept disappearing behind the image he couldn't shift – that of Ethan's dead face laughing at him. He had to speak; the silence felt as if it was clogging his skin, filling his nostrils. 'Put the driver on the phone.'

'Does that mean you have come to the correct conclusion?'

'It means that I have a way of moving things forward. I'm going to share each address one at a time so I can monitor your progress. Keep track of delivery and times. If I get the slightest sense that you're not on schedule, I'll be obliged to employ some support staff. That's it. It's non-negotiable. Now, do as I said, put the driver on the phone.'

Calvin hardened his tone and this time he heard Ethan's breathing change. Briefly, two breaths, just a couple of seconds, and then his voice returned, confident as before.

'I can live with that.'

'Can you?'

'Easily.' A slight pause. Although they were miles apart, it felt to Calvin as if they were staring into each other's eyes. He made a point of not blinking. 'There is one other thing,' Ethan said. 'Before I hand the phone over, there is one more requirement. Something that will be easy for you to do, as long as your ego doesn't get in the way.'

'And what might that be?'

'I'm going to tell you. And once you agree we can get this show back on the road…'

Ethan Hall continued to talk. Calvin Brent listened in silence. This time his mind was clear and computed the options with ease. He decided even before Ethan had finished that it was a surprisingly harmless request. In fact, if anything, Calvin reasoned, it strengthened his own hand.

'I can do that for you,' he said when the time came. 'No problem at all.'

'Good. I'm pleased. The next voice will be the driver's.'

Calvin heard the muffled noise of the phone being transferred and nodded in satisfaction. He allowed himself to smile.

So did Ethan Hall.

28

Anne-Marie Wells couldn't help but wonder if all terminally ill people saved their most honest smile for the times they were alone. She certainly did. It was a smile impossible to categorise, spawned by the knowledge that death was growing remorselessly inside her. For reasons she didn't fully understand, it made Anne-Marie think of bedtime.

'But it isn't bedtime yet,' she said. 'I don't feel anything like tired enough.'

Only that was never the criteria for being sent to bed. Every child knew that. Bedtime was a seemingly arbitrary moment chosen by parents, a time only ever brought forward as a punishment, only ever extended as a most special treat.

'I don't feel tired enough at the moment.' Anne-Marie felt obliged to add the qualification. The time when she could take her energy level for granted seemed a long time ago. Now it had occasional, unexpected highs and ever increasing lows. 'I don't know if that's because my energy is travelling on the back of my emotions,' she said, 'and my emotions are all over the place. I don't know if that's it, or if it's just the physical weakness caused by the cancer, or if it's a combination of the two.

'What you discover once you know you are dying of cancer is that up until then you have always been able to forget things, whether bad or good, even if only for a short while. Cancer never lets you forget. It's there, with you constantly, in your mind as much as anywhere else, even when you're asleep. It's always pulling and dragging and draining, filling the space between your subconscious and your conscious. There's nothing you can do and nowhere you can go to forget it. Even when you smile. It shapes everything.'

Anne-Marie frowned and took a step forwards. The vision in front of her was in danger of disappearing. She concentrated hard. She willed the edges and the detail to come back into focus. It took a second or two. She waited impatiently until clarity returned, until the muscles in the face showed life and the skin coloured.

'It doesn't mean it's inside you now,' she said. 'In fact, I'm sure it's not. I'm sure we can keep sharing like this and your experience will be as pure and perfect as it was the first time. I really need you to believe that.'

I really need you to.

Anne-Marie felt the plea come out of her before she heard it. She saw the younger version of herself, the girl about to become a woman, accept the role she had been summoned to play with unquestionable grace. She had first appeared some weeks earlier when Anne-Marie had woken screaming in response to a nightmare. She had been there even before Marcus, offering herself as the reminder of a different time and a different way of being. She was, Anne-Marie would have said if asked the question, purely a figment of her imagination. Yet she welcomed her nonetheless.

'I'm obviously desperate,' she said, 'and I know that when I die, you will too. Or maybe we'll both live together? Can you answer that?'

The vision raised both hands, palms upwards, and gestured into the open space of the lounge. Anne-Marie's gaze followed their direction. The room, like the rest of the rented house, was not hers. The wallpaper, the furniture, the carpet, the lighting were all neutral and hardwearing, chosen by someone else to minimize wear and tear. Everything here was simply marking time from one passer-by to the next; the place more of a routeway than a home, better to look out of the window at the view than look down and risk seeing road kill.

A quote by Susan Sontag, an American writer and activist who had long been a source of inspiration, popped unbidden into Anne-Marie's mind:

'Life is a movie; death is a photograph.'

There it was then. The answer. Flicked to the fore of her consciousness by a question asked in a soulless room.

Death is a photograph.

She would have argued that point once upon a time; at least to some degree. She would have argued that all time – past, present and future – and all beliefs could be seen and sensed within the stillness and apparent isolation of a brilliantly taken image. She would have likened a photo to a door leading into another world.

'But perhaps it's a door leading out, not leading in?' Anne-Marie turned back to face her younger self. 'I'd never considered that before. I think I – we – always believed in the sun and the bright, blue sky. I think we drew our strength from that, even when taking pictures of darkness. I think that is still what you believe in, isn't it?'

The vision smiled gently, inclining her head.

'I am going to take that photo, the self-portrait,' Anne-Marie said. 'I've decided. My mind is made up. Whether or not I call it *Dying* or *Processing* or something else altogether we'll wait and see. I'm sure the title is inside me somewhere, so it's bound to come out. The best way to reveal it is to commit myself to the process, to look closely through the lens and let my professionalism, or my instinct – or you! – show me what it is I'm really looking at, what the story is really all about. I need to be sure that you are with me, though. I know it's selfish of me, but I want us to share everything that lies ahead together. Can we do that?'

The vision offered a hand and Anne-Marie reached out instinctively to take it. It felt as if her movement shattered a wall of glass. She flinched, squeezing her eyes shut and raising her shoulders protectively. She realised within a split-second that her mind was playing tricks. When she opened her eyes, the vision had disappeared.

Anne-Marie smiled.

29

Peter Jones curled his lips in what DS Kevin McNeill took to be a silent and somewhat threatening invitation. Then he nodded abruptly, listened to some more and nodded again. A few seconds later he nodded a third time. Standing only one metre away, Kevin could sense the intense focus with which his boss was receiving the news. He waited for the phone conversation to end. It did so with a terse 'Good job' and the slightest quizzical frown. Kevin knew better than to speak first.

'We've got our first possible break,' Peter said. 'Detective Constable Benson met half an hour ago with an informant who says Ethan Hall is staying with him. The story is Hall made a beeline for the informant as soon as he broke out of hospital. If the story is to be believed they were good mates years ago, before Hall came to our attention.'

'You don't sound too confident, boss.'

'Just gut instinct,' Peter shrugged, 'something tugging at my innards. Having said that, it's still definitely worth prioritising and acting on with our usual mix of extreme urgency and extreme care. After all, it's a quick result and if it turns out to be a proper result, well, we'd all welcome that.' He forced a smile. 'Look, maybe it's great Intel and I'm doubting it because I'm not feeling lucky today. Maybe it's as simple as that.'

'Your gut instinct hasn't let us down yet.'

'Has it not?'

Kevin shifted his weight from foot to foot, just as he'd seen people do under interrogation in the witness box. He knew better than to avoid, deny or adapt the truth with this man. *Everyone knows you're a lucky copper. For some reason you always get the break just when you need it.*

Before he could decide what to say, Peter continued, 'Don't confuse gut instinct with good luck. As I've said to you before, if you've done enough high level training and you keep testing that training under real-life pressure, you're gut instinct – your intuition, call it what you will, – will develop naturally. The trick lies in being able to recognise it, interpret it accurately and then use it to guide your decision-making. Right?'

'Yes, boss.' Kevin straightened. Sometimes his DCI had a look in his eyes that made you think he knew precisely what you were thinking. That look was there now. Kevin resisted the temptation to check the knot in his tie. Instead he tried to force all thoughts of *lucky copper* out of his mind. It wasn't easy, especially under such scrutiny.

Jones maintained the silence for a few seconds before the merest grin played on his face and then he said, 'If, as detectives, we combine our gut instinct with a tried and tested process and a willingness to think and act outside the box whenever the situation demands it, we become more and more likely to make our own luck.'

His mobile rang again. Kevin watched him take it out of his inside pocket, glance at the screen and reject the call without hesitation. 'Sometimes,' he said, a sudden far-away look in his eyes, 'the better we get as coppers the worse we might become in other ways.'

Now it seemed to Kevin that their roles had reversed abruptly. Peter's shoulders sagged briefly. His face lined with an obvious and quickly disguised weary acceptance of pain.

He's trying to hide from me!

The realisation made Kevin feel surprisingly awkward. As Peter replaced the phone he shook his head and exhaled forcefully. The weariness disappeared. Almost.

'So. Let's focus on what needs to be done. I want you to liaise with Benson. The informant lives in the Meadows. His name's Darren Smith. Deals drugs and does whatever else he can to eke out a living and a low-level reputation. Let's get everyone in place as we usually would. Make sure everyone understands the need for us to be super-cautious. We have to work on the premise that Ethan will spot things anyone else would miss.'

'What if he leaves the place whilst they're watching?'

'I don't think he will. If he's there – or wherever he is – I'm sure he's going to stay holed up.'

'You don't think he's got plans?'

'I'm sure he's got plans. I just can't see how he can execute them. He doesn't have the contacts or the experience. Being hunted now that everyone knows his name and what he looks like is a whole new world to him. He can't go from A to B and hypnotise everyone who sees him into forgetting his face.'

'Are you sure, boss?'

'We're well and truly fucked if he can.' Peter remembered Patrick's memory loss. 'No, however unusual Ethan is – however dangerous – he's going to have his limits just like the rest of us. If we do our job right, we get him. That's the bottom line.'

'Amen to that.'

'I don't want us relying on prayers! Focus on procedures and professionalism. Just make sure everyone's on the top of their game. The bad guys always come to us sooner or later. You know that as well as I do. And it's as true for Ethan Hall as it is for the rest of them. Let's just make it sooner rather than later.'

'I'll contact DC Benson straight away, pass on your warnings.'

'Good.'

'Can I just ask you…'

'What?'

'Why you're not going over there and getting hands on?'

'Don't you think Benson can do it?

'Yes, but we all know you like to be where the action is. And it's even easier to imagine that would be the case where Ethan Hall is concerned.'

'Maybe the lesson is you should never presume.'

'Understood, boss. Right, I'll get to it.'

Peter raised his hand, temporarily halting Kevin's departure. 'Find out everything you can about this Smith character. I really don't get the connection between him and Ethan. And if they are so tight, I don't understand why Smith is so keen to turn him in.'

'Will do. Although…'

'What?'

'You said the guy will do whatever he can to make a living. Maybe he's desperate for the cash or needs to get in Benson's good books, or both?'

'Yeah. Maybe. I can't help but think, though, that if you really knew Ethan Hall, if you were really aware of what he's capable of, you'd need to have a bloody good reason to betray him.'

'Greed is as good a motive as any, boss. Maybe Smith is seeing it as easy money? Besides, from our point of view if everything works out, it's just one action and we've got him. We hit the house swift and hard and Hall's back in custody.'

'Let's hope so. OK. Get on with it. This needs to be seamless and silent. Keep me updated.'

'All the way.'

Peter waited until the DS had gone before taking out his phone. One new voice message. Just as expected. It was easy to guess the content and the tone. It would be a call for a meeting, an essential possibly relationship-saving meeting, delivered in a voice that combined anger and threat with undisguised fear, a voice verging on hysteria. Nic's voice.

Peter looked at the phone. The same old thought played through his mind.

Sometimes you just don't have a choice.

Only people who worked in the emergency services understood that. It was the secret knowledge shared by those who were paid to keep everyone else safe and well. Once you had chosen a career that required you to prioritise the greater good, sooner or later you were faced with what outsiders would regard as the most difficult choice. And they was most 50% right and 50% wrong in their assessment. Yes, it would be difficult. But, no, it wasn't a choice. Sometimes you had to do the job you were paid to do no matter what the personal cost or risk. Sometimes choice didn't enter into it.

This was one of those times. It was not the first. And, Peter considered ruefully, it would not be the last. It was the price he paid for putting the words *Detective Chief Inspector* in front of his name.

He raised the phone to his ear and listened to the message. Just in case his instinct was wrong. Just in case it was some other news and life at home was going on as it once had.

The message carried on for longer than was needed. As he had guessed it would. The mix of emotions and the hope of a sudden response stretched the narrative until eventually the words dried up. They were followed by an unnecessarily long silence before the phone went dead.

Peter texted his reply.

Can't talk now. Sorry. I will be able to talk tonight. I will be home as early as possible. Promise.

He sent the message, returned the phone to his pocket and forced himself to think about Ethan Hall. About what needed to be done if he and his team were going to keep people safe, if they were going to get a quick result. He thought about procedures and professionalism. About creativity and luck. He drilled the thoughts through his head. Repeatedly. Until his focus had returned and nothing else mattered. He looked to his right, imagining that Kevin was still there. 'It's a mantra for the work-obsessed,' he explained. 'It's the alternative for those who can't pray.'

30

Diane Clusker had told him it was a miracle. She said that was the only word that could describe her experience. It was a miracle and he was a miracle worker. She was sure of it. How else, she asked as she left his office, could you possibly explain the transformation that had taken place? After all, she had arrived feeling suicidal and was leaving brimming with hope. If that wasn't a miracle, what was?

Marcus Kline chose not to answer. Rather than explain to her about the power of words and touch, of how tone of voice, timing and sequencing could be used to exercise the subconscious and influence the brain, he simply thanked her for giving him the chance to help and reinforced the message that he was always available should she ever need to see him again.

Diane had squeezed his right hand and promised she would pray for him. 'Every night, starting tonight, until that evil, evil man is captured,' she said. 'It's the least I can do.'

'Thank you,' he had said. And he had meant it. He really was grateful. Not for the prayers, of course, but for the sincerity and willingness to help. Not too long ago he would have considered it to be proof only of the power of reciprocity. He would have dismissed it as an inevitable response to the fact that she was clearly in his debt, her attitude a consequence of his skill rather than an indication of her caring nature.

Now, though, Marcus felt genuinely moved. More than that he felt guilty that his motivation for helping Diane had been selfish rather than altruistic. She had provided an unexpected, and much needed, opportunity to make himself feel useful again. Their time together had proven to be of at least as much value to him as it had to her. And, for the first time in his life, a part of him wished he believed in miracles.

He shrugged the thought away. If anything was a clear indication that he was psychologically and emotionally weak right now, that was it. Rather than hand over responsibility he needed to create some miracles of his own, the sort that could only be accomplished by human talent and skill not by prayer and the abdication of effort.

That, he realised, was what his subconscious had been telling him when it had urged him to take the fight to Ethan Hall, when it had spurred him to share his story with the reporter Dave Johnson. For the first time in his adult life, he could now do something useful – in fact, the most useful thing he could ever do – on behalf of everyone else and not just himself. If he was going to win he could do it only by forgetting Marcus Kline and the associated brand image. This time his focus, determination and strength would come from thinking solely of others. For the first time in a long time, Marcus felt a genuine fizz of excitement and energy shoot through his system.

As he watched Diane Clusker walking away from his office, passing the Galleries of Justice on her way back towards the bus station, he felt like shouting after her, 'Thank you for reminding me! Until today I'd forgotten about the others!'

Only before he could say anything an instantly recognisable voice in his head asked, 'Even me?' And the energy collapsed back into his gut like a heavy weight.

'No Simon, I never forgot you.' He said the words out loud, turning back into the office, letting the door close behind him. 'How could you ever think that?'

The silence dared him to answer his own question. It was all too easy. This time his words were an apology.

'OK. I never forgot you, it's just that sometimes – too many times – I thought about me first. I somehow managed to entangle doing good work for others with making sure it was always rewarding for the Marcus Kline brand. I've always cared about others. It's just that whatever I did, my ego was always front and centre. I thought I was the best, you see? I needed to believe that. Now I know I'm not. And I know it should never have mattered. Anne-Marie always said, if you're good enough to help someone then you're good enough and that's all you have to be. Only I didn't pay her any attention. I had to be acknowledged as the world's number one. I always thought it was the most important achievement. Now it feels like it was just a safety net. One that Ethan Hall's ripped away.'

A slight pause.

Then Marcus continued, 'I would have done anything in my power to save you. Honestly. No matter what the cost. This isn't what I ever imagined. It's just that I have to save Anne-Marie and Peter and maybe even other people I don't actually know from whatever it is Ethan Hall is planning. I can't do that if I'm not functioning at my best, if I don't prioritise my own performance, if I don't fight. And I'm finding that a struggle. I'm having to focus on me in ways I never have before. So I'm sorry you've been out of my thoughts for a while. I hope you understand.'

As his words ended Marcus realised how still his body had become. He looked round the empty reception; imagined Emma smiling and shaking her head. A part of him wished she was still sitting there. A bigger part was delighted she had left when she did. At least now there was one less person to worry about, one less possible disaster to be responsible for.

His eyes watered. The stillness in the room was compelling, cloying. He could feel it seeking to hold him in place. He could feel himself breathing it in.

I need to move!

Marcus forced himself to set the alarm and step outside. He closed the door, feeling its reassuring weight as it swung inwards, letting his hand rest upon it as it sealed the entrance.

The idea came so unexpectedly it made him gasp. He responded to it without hesitation, afraid that thoughts would only get in the way. He began to walk, faster than normal, drawing in the city air with great deliberateness, blinking away the tears.

He reached The Cross Keys within two minutes. He pushed through the door and stepped into the bar. Shades of brown dominated with the wooden floor and wooden tables and the bar itself, curving slightly at one end. The room was empty save for a group of elderly men sat at a table by the far wall and a much younger man leaning against the bar. The group was talking politics. The young man was chatting to one of the barmaids.

Marcus moved to the other end of the bar, to the curve, and removed a five pound note from his wallet. His heart was pounding. The second barmaid was with him in an instant, smiling as if he was a regular. Marcus ordered a pint of New Dawn Pale, Simon's favourite drink. As he waited for the beer to be pulled he couldn't help but glance at the table where Simon used to sit. He had no intention of sitting there; just being in the place was enough for now. After Simon's death he had vowed never to come back in. It had been a stupid, petulant response, as if the pub was the only thing that would remind him of his loss and his selfishness. As if the office didn't. As if a mirror didn't.

Marcus took his beer, did his best to return the young woman's ever-present smile, and chose the table furthest away from the other customers. He took a sip of his pale, golden liquid and looked again at Simon's empty table. The beer was not fully to his taste but that really wasn't the point. He wasn't sure yet if this was a good idea or a bad idea, but that really wasn't the point either. The most important thing was that this was an idea turned into action. And action cured fear.

As Marcus stared at the table he imagined Simon sitting there, early morning, eating breakfast, chatting to Cassandra, the barmaid he had started dating shortly before his death. He remembered how Emma had teased and tormented Simon about his newly found love interest. He remembered how he had stood by silently as the young man tried to deny it.

'Why can't you just tell it like it is?' Emma had asked. 'Why is it that men struggle to be honest in matters of the heart?'

Simon blushed. 'Don't you dare stereotype! Men are as varied in their responses to all aspects of life as you complicated and amazing women!'

'Stop trying to change the topic by shifting it away from yourself and broadening the context,' Emma laughed, 'that's a typical Marcus ploy and I know it too well to fall for it. So, come on, answer the question.'

'Ok, then, I will. In matters of the heart, as you so delicately refer to them as, indeed, with all other types of relationships, simple straightforward honesty is rarely if ever the best policy.'

'What? I cannot believe you're saying this!'

'It shouldn't come as any surprise.'

'Why not?'

'Because my mentor here,' Simon waved a hand in Marcus's direction, 'has gone to considerable lengths to instil in me that very fact. Straightforward honesty isn't a method employed by the highly trained professional communicator, whereas well packaged honesty is.'

'We're talking about personal relationships of the most

important kind, not work!' It was Emma's turn to redden as her teasing began to give way to anger. 'No woman expects, wants or even needs deliberately planned professional communication from her partner. Honesty is a sign of commitment and trust and sharing and all those things that show love! Or hasn't your mentor taught you that yet?'

'In case you've forgotten we are in our workplace now,' Simon said. 'I am here to behave as a professional and to learn and practise my craft. To do anything else would be to take advantage of the boss's time and money. And – and this is the most important part – it's you that I wasn't being open and honest with and you're not my partner.' Simon beamed, his confidence restored. 'That, I think you will agree, is game, set and match to me!'

Emma whooped with joy, her anger dissolving as quickly as it had appeared. 'Only a man can think he's won when he has so clearly lost!'

'What are you talking about?'

'The point of this conversation was to make you admit how you felt about Cassandra,' Emma said, 'not justify your use of well packaged honesty – which, as an aside, I didn't think was that well packaged at all. And you have indeed just admitted you think of her as your partner! So, the game is actually mine!'

'Only in your dreams!' Simon retorted. 'I never said anything about Cassandra. Throughout this I have only ever being talking theoretically and hypothetically. All you are doing now is showing how desperate you are to feel superior.'

'Only men feel the need for superiority! Women are far too busy trying to hold the world together...'

Marcus took another sip of his beer and used it to try and clear the memory. It seemed such a long time ago. A lifetime.

A time when he had been certain of everything, a time before doubt, a time when fear had been another word for fun.

Marcus drank some more beer, fighting the pull of the empty table. As he was doing so, a woman entered the bar. He was grateful for the brief distraction. He used his peripheral vision to observe her, letting his professional mind come to the fore, making its immediate assessment.

She was five feet eight inches tall, with short mousey brown hair in need of a good, professional cut. She was wearing a short, scuffed brown leather jacket, an old pair of Levi jeans and a pair of training shoes in need of a wash. She was skinny with pale skin and light blue eyes that matched the colour of the vein standing out in her neck. Her eyes were open too wide and yet, from his perspective, they clearly saw very little, blinkered he was sure by some great, constant, urgency and something more – a shadow, heavy and frightening, pressing down on her conscious with suffocating force. A trauma from her past, he reasoned, or maybe, judging by the way her breathing came from high in her chest making her movements sharp and jerky, a series of traumas. She was definitely a single woman. A smoker. A drug taker. A heavy drinker – of cheap, strong booze, the sort that burns and rots your insides. In all likelihood she was an occasional prostitute. Easy to read.

He watched her order a large measure of the house vodka, drain it in one go and order a second. It was then she saw him. She did the kind of obvious double take most people do when they see someone famous in a place they don't expect. Only seeing him forced her breathing even higher. It activated the flight-fight-or freeze response. Even though she didn't know he was watching her. Even though she had nothing the be scared of.

Marcus kept his vertical vision low as if looking at his beer, watching her struggling to come to a decision; fighting to make herself do whatever she felt was right.

The second vodka helped her. Downed just like the first, she returned the empty glass to the bar top before taking the two steps necessary to reach his table.

'You're Marcus Kline.'

It was the second time he had been told that in a matter of hours. Only this woman wasn't a reporter, and she clearly wasn't a reader of his books or a business leader needing his professional help. He was careful to soften his face when he looked up at her.

'Yes,' he said. 'How can I help you?'

'That monster, Ethan Hall,' she said, unable to look at him for more than a split-second, her eyes flittering around the room, glancing out of the windows. 'I just want to say the next time the police catch him they need to put a bullet in his black heart. They need to kill the bastard! They need to kill him stone dead for what he does to people!'

She turned abruptly, giving him no time to speak, and rushed out of the pub. Marcus made no attempt to follow her. No one else seemed to have noticed their brief interaction. The old men were still engrossed in their own conversation. The young man and the barmaid were still oblivious to the rest of the world.

Marcus didn't know why the woman had said what she did. The most likely reason was that she had seen the story in the news and wanted to express her feelings. Only it had seemed more personal than that. She had sounded more like an angry, helpless and ignored victim than a social spectator who believed in execution. Once that insight would have been enough to make him get involved. He would have tried to prevent her from leaving, or at least gone after her. Today that just hadn't felt right. He needed to focus his energy on what he knew for sure was happening. Besides, by the time he looked out of the window the woman had disappeared.

As people do.

Marcus tried the beer again. It really wasn't to his taste. He pushed it away.

After Simon's death, Cassandra had left for pastures unknown. Just like Emma. He, on the other hand, was staying here, in his hometown, with his wife. He had problems to solve and he was going to solve them all.

Marcus left his unfinished beer on the table and walked out of the bar. He pushed away the lingering thoughts about the woman and imagined instead just how he was going to draw Ethan Hall out and capture him. And how he was going to save his wife from cancer. The notion of failure was terrifying, so he kept walking.

Action, he told himself again, cures fear.

31

Nicholas Evans knew something had to happen. More precisely, something had to change. Only he didn't want to let his fear and his anger force him into an action from which there would be no turning back; an action he would regret for the rest of his life.

So Nic was doing his best to control his emotions. It was almost impossible, but he was still hanging in there, clinging for all he was worth, using a level of strength and self-discipline he hadn't known he possessed. Clinging like a man holding on to a precipice and feeling his fingers losing their grip one by one, a man treating every second as if it was the most precious thing in the world, a man who could only be saved by a strong pair of hands reaching down and hauling him back to terra firma.

The truth was the decision that needed to be made, the decision that would determine the action he took, was not a one-person decision. It would come out of dialogue. At least, in an ideal world it would. Ideally it would grow from a sharing of truths and perspectives, from heartfelt communication and genuine concern each for the other. If, after all of that, the decision they came to was that the end had been reached, then at least it would have been reached in the best possible way.

Nic shuddered at the prospect. He didn't want an ending of any sort; not the grown-up sharing of actualities and inevitabilities, and certainly not the isolated despair of realising there wasn't even a conversation to be had. The worst of all worlds would be to have to do this alone, to end something so special unnoticed and unsupported, to fall without anyone watching, to scream without being heard.

Nic's phone buzzed. He picked it up from the coffee table and saw the text from Peter. He read it far more slowly than he needed to. It was not the response he had wanted, but it was a response nonetheless. More than that there was a promise to talk.

I will be home as early as possible.

It was an acknowledgement of their need; well, of Nic's anyway. And it was a commitment, even though it was wrapped in the vague as-and-when timings Peter only ever offered when he was on a case. Timings that often drifted from one day to the next, from one week to another. But surely that wasn't going to happen today, not with their relationship so close to collapse, when every second mattered?

As early as possible.

Better than nothing. Much better. He could have been ignored, but instead he had received a message, a sign that meant Peter was still there. A sign that said *Hold on, I'm on my way.*

Just knowing that was enough to give him the strength.

Surely?

Nic replaced the phone on the coffee table and sat back in the armchair, reflecting on how good their relationship had once been and how it had changed.

The problem hadn't been caused by Ethan Hall's escape from the hospital. It had started before then, on the night Anne-Marie had phoned Peter calling for him to save Marcus. Right there and then Nic had seen his partner transform in a way he could never have imagined, in a way that had terrified him. The image was still in the forefront of Nic's mind, so clear it was undeniable.

A Komodo dragon.

A cold-hearted hunter at the top of its food chain. That's what he had seen. His partner was not just the loving, gentle man who had said 'Forever'. He was also that…that thing. Possibly, and this was the most terrifying thought of all, he was only that. Possibly everything else was the lie, the disguise he used to fit in and get along.

Nic pressed his head back into the chair. The questions thudding. What if he had fallen in love with the disguise and not the real man? What did that mean about him?

Answer: that he was so desperate to be loved he couldn't see the truth.

What future could they possible have together?

Answer: none.

What, then, of the rest of his life?

Answer: a rapid descent into loneliness and despair.

Nic closed his eyes. Everything had seemed so safe. So perfect. How could it possibly have been so close to disaster at the same time? How could he not have noticed? His fingers gripped the arms of the chair. His heart pounded. The most important question of all kept hammering inside him: *Just what are you holding on to?*

It was the question he couldn't – daren't – answer. As he fought to ignore it the doorbell rang. For a brief moment his heart leaped as he thought it was Peter and then he realised he would have just let himself in. By the time he reached the door his focus was on dissolving his disappointment and looking as if everything was normal. That's why he didn't peer through the small glass panel to check the visitor in the way Peter always insisted he should.

Instead he opened the door without thinking about it. He said, 'Hello. How can I help you?' without studying the person fully. By then it was way too late.

'You can't help me,' the visitor said. 'I'm actually here to help you. Aren't you going to invite me in?'

'Of course,' Nic answered without hesitation, as if it was the most natural thing in the world. He let the visitor close the door behind him and then led the way into the lounge. Ethan Hall followed without saying a word.

32

Peter Jones wanted to make as much noise as possible. Noise and movement, if directed and coordinated appropriately, always brought the hunted out into the open. Peter had known that for decades. He had learnt it as a boy when his father had taken him on his first shoot.

Peter had grown up in the country and in many ways he still missed the simple village life. He felt that it, rather than city living, was the original backbone of the nation. More than that, he had realised a long time ago that a backbone was only as secure as everything else around it. Nothing existed in isolation. Everything was part of an interactive system. That was the most important lesson nature offered. Everything connects, even if you can't always see the connections. Even if the flow of cause and effect takes time to manifest.

That meant the security and future of village life, his national backbone, was determined by what was happening around it, in the towns and cities. That was one of the reasons why he became a police officer. He knew that, if left unchecked, unacceptable noise and movement spreads. Criminals always seek to expand their areas of influence, to create an ever-greater domain. What starts in the city doesn't stay there unless it's contained or curtailed. The best way to do that was to organise specific, targeted noise and movement, to control the environment and drive your prey into a trap of your own making.

On those rare occasions when he had the free time, Peter still went beating. It was the job his father had taught him as a young boy, how to flush birds such as pheasant or partridge from cover and into the line of fire of the waiting guns.

Beating was an essential part of every shoot, and it had to be done well if the shoot was to be successful. Beaters worked as part of a team, often using their own well-trained dogs as support. Every shoot ground was divided into areas of countryside known as drives. The shoot manager decided which way he wanted the birds to fly and directed the beaters accordingly. The people with guns, those paying for the shoot, were then lined up along the edge of this drive whilst Peter and his fellow beaters created a line along the opposite end of the drive. Their job was to move forward towards the guns, maintaining the line, investigating every bit of natural cover, creating disciplined disturbance.

And the process needed to be disciplined throughout because there was always the potential for things to go wrong. If the line became uneven, if beaters took detours to avoid difficult undergrowth, if anyone stopped briefly for a chat, if the line moved too quickly or if some dogs became over-excited the birds could easily escape. Sometimes they would do so by staying on the ground and running back unnoticed between the beaters. Sometimes they would be startled into all taking flight at once and the shooters would find themselves firing at a great cloud of birds, having the opportunity to bring down only one or two.

When the beating was at its best however, when instructions were clear and the line managed its movement and noise well, the birds were flushed into the air in smaller, more easily targeted groups. Sometimes beaters would wave a coloured flag making the birds fly higher, giving the shooters more time to choose and hit their targets.

Peter loved beating. Not just because it took him back to his roots, but also because it was a team activity. There always more birds than there were men and dogs; the birds, though, were incapable of planned coordination. Even when they all moved as one, they were still essentially acting as panicked individuals. A small, well-managed team moving at the right pace in the right direction, making the right sort of noise always flushed out their target. And once they had them out in the open – bang! – they were quickly brought down to earth.

Noise and movement.

That, in part, was what he was paid to create and coordinate. Identify the culprit then flush them out. Or, in this case, create enough disturbance in the right places to ensure that either someone revealed Ethan Hall's hiding place, or he felt the need to make a run for it.

Peter had his own team – his personally selected *beaters* – plus the support of a specifically commissioned Criminal Analyst and a couple of computer techies. The Analyst, a woman he had worked with before, was excellent at studying the incoming information, determining its credibility and creating link charts that showed lines of connectivity between relevant individuals and/or behaviours. Peter was keeping in touch with her on a regular basis.

Media stories about Ethan's escape and the threat he posed had clearly struck a chord. The public had been, and still were, offering all sorts of feedback. So far it varied from the possible to the absurd. Ethan had been seen supposedly throughout the city and in other parts of the country. One man had even phoned in from Tenerife, where he had just arrived on holiday, to say he was sure that Ethan had been disguised as cabin crew.

It had, though, been Peter's visits to other police stations, talking directly to detectives there, that had created the potential breakthrough. The call from DC Brian Benson saying he had an address where Hall was supposed to be staying should have sparked a thrill of anticipation. Only it hadn't. Somehow Peter just couldn't see it. More importantly, he couldn't feel it. Even though he couldn't argue logically with Kevin McNeill's observation that criminals always looked after themselves first and foremost and would do just about anything for easy money.

Peter was used to looking at a terrain filled with birds and not being able to see one of them. He understood that even if your target wasn't in plain sight it could still be almost underneath your feet. So you had to have your line of beaters ready and your line of guns in the right place. You had to act based on what you had been told, not on what you could see at that precise moment in time. You had to make sure that if your target was there, you flushed it out according to plan, that you drove it in the right direction, that it simply couldn't escape.

Right now everything was in place. McNeill had passed on the necessary messages. Benson had assumed control. He had, in turn, brought in the specialist team who would make the arrest. Peter knew the drill. He knew the roles individuals would play and the tactics they would employ. He knew how the team would function. It was, as McNeill had said, a situation he had organised and managed many times.

A couple of officers would have taken up temporary residence in a terraced house opposite Darren's. It was usually an easy thing to arrange. Many people were willing to offer the police a room and regular cups of tea and a promise of secrecy, at least in the short-term. In Peter's experience, people who welcomed you into their home wanted to feel the excitement of being part of something they would usually only see on the television; they wanted to be able to tell family, friends and neighbours they had played their part in a dangerous police operation. Hosting a surveillance team didn't make you a hero, but it could make some people feel like one. And by the time those individuals had perfected their story, they would have at least convinced themselves if not others that they truly were.

The specialist team – the raid team as it was known – would be waiting for some agreed signal that Ethan was in the house. They were trained to hit hard and fast, and they would need to do that against Ethan Hall.

Keep your eyes low, head down, Peter thought. *Shout. Scream. Make lots of noise. Do everything you can to scramble the bastard's brain, to stop him from looking at you or talking to you.*

Noise and movement.

The keys to success where Ethan Hall was concerned.

Only, no matter how much he wanted for Ethan to be in Smith's house, for this to be it, he couldn't really bring himself to believe. If he had, he would have been there himself. He wouldn't have left the arrest of Ethan to someone else. McNeill had been absolutely right to question his reasons for staying away. He had been absolutely right, too, not to push the point any further.

Peter checked his watch. Something should have happened by now. He paced his office. He had to direct his mind somewhere and if it didn't go towards Ethan Hall it turned inevitably towards Nic. He found it much easier to visualise how that was playing out. Their relationship was so fragile they had to create some quality time together; time to begin the rebuilding process, time in which to reassure Nic that the professional Peter Jones would eventually be put to rest forever and until then, no matter how it might seem on occasion, he was still Peter's ultimate love.

Even if it was far more complicated than that. Even if, where Peter was concerned, the notion of ultimate was open to serious debate. Lovers expected to be at the top of their partner's emotional hierarchy. It was a more than reasonable expectation. The often unspoken requirement and associated understanding went something like, *I know you will love other people and maybe other things in powerful and different ways, just make sure no love is the same as, or exceeds, the love you feel for me.* That was the silent deal and anyway you looked at it, it was a more than fair request from someone offering to share their one and only life with you.

So how could you possibly ask your partner to accept the fact you loved your work as much you loved them? That for the relationship to work they had to be willing to share you completely, sometimes, even, take second place. How do you square that particular circle?

Peter thought of Mike Coopland, a dear friend and the most successful and charismatic barrister he knew. The pair had worked together on several high profile and challenging cases. Mike could weave together and deliver a compelling story in ways that usually had a jury eating out of his hands. He was a master of his craft, a man who revelled in the cut and thrust of the courtroom. Yet Peter doubted if even Mike could successfully defend his position to Nic. Some stories required the listener to make a great leap of faith and, to make matters worse, to do so whilst carrying a significant burden. That was the type of story he was having to manage now.

'Christ, I need Ethan Hall to be locked up! I need this to be over!'

Peter's phone rang. It was Benson.

'Yes?' Peter heard his own voice cold and hard, the sudden rush of adrenaline blocked behind it. 'What have you got for me?'

'It's bad news I'm afraid. He wasn't there.'

As expected.

'No sign at all?'

'No. We checked everything thoroughly.'

'So we don't know if he was ever there?'

'I'm sure he was.'

'Why?'

'The way my CHIS reacted. It was like he was scared and relieved and confused all at the same time. I'm sure Ethan had been with him and I'm convinced he didn't expect him to leave. The best I can suggest is that something happened to spook Ethan and he took off in the nick of time.'

Peter considered briefly. CHIS was the correct term for a person more commonly referred to as an informant. It stood for Covert Human Intelligence Source. In this case Peter couldn't help but wonder about the nature of the intelligence, and about the motivation of the man delivering it.

'Tell me more about your source.'

'There's nothing much to add from what I said before. He's served some time for dealing. He'll do anything to make money as long as it isn't too risky. He denies it but I'm sure he's connected, albeit near the bottom of the chain, to Calvin Brent.'

'Do you think he would have told Brent that Ethan Hall was staying with him?'

'There's no reason to think so. Hall wasn't there for long. I find it hard to believe that in such a relatively short space of time he would have told Brent and then come running to me. I think my man is scared of Ethan and wanted rid of him. So when he heard about the reward he figured he could kill two birds with one stone.'

'Maybe. It's certainly a plausible explanation, one that would explain Ethan's disappearance.'

'How's that?'

'There's no way your man could decide to sell Ethan to you without him sensing something bad was happening. Ethan Hall is not a man you keep secrets from.'

'But, again, he wouldn't have had much time to work it out.'

'Ethan Hall only needs to look at you. He needs a fraction of a second to get inside your head. Trust me, you've never met anyone like him and I hope you never do.'

'Well, if that's true,' Peter heard the doubt in the other man's voice, 'how come he didn't punish my man for betraying him? After all he has a track record for violence.'

'That's a very good question,' Peter admitted. 'The only possible answer I've got right now is that he couldn't have known how long he'd got before we turned up, so he prioritised just getting out of there.'

'Does that mean my guy could be at risk?'

'For sure. Ethan Hall has a vindictive streak. He certainly won't forgive or forget. The thing is, he now hasn't got anywhere he can hide. That was his bolthole. He wouldn't have wanted to give it up and he's had to. So we have to ask ourselves, where does he go from there?'

'Maybe he's running blind, in a state of panic. He's just discovered he couldn't trust the friend he chose to go to, so even if he knows some other people he's going to be distrustful at the very least. Maybe this has messed with his head and he isn't currently the threat you believe him to be.'

Peter noted the deliberate use of the word believe. He chose to ignore it. Benson wasn't part of his own team and in all probability this was the closest he would ever come to confronting Ethan.

'Keep in contact with your man until this is over,' he said. 'Make it clear to him that he needs to get in touch with you if he hears anything even vaguely relevant. Tell him, too, he should consider himself at risk until Ethan is back in custody. That might help keep him safe and increase the chances of him sharing any new information. Got that?'

'Absolutely.'

'Good. Well done today. Maybe next time.'

Peter ended the call. The more he thought about it, the more sense it made that Ethan would have spotted his so-called friend's intention to turn him in. Smith was lucky the synesthete hadn't stayed to take his revenge. Now, though, the two big questions still remained; questions that were, if anything, highlighted by the team's recent near miss.

Question 1: Just what the hell was Ethan Hall planning to do next?

And

Question 2: Where was he right now?

33

Ethan Hall was in the lounge of Peter and Nic's three bedroomed detached home in Burton Joyce, a large village seven miles east of Nottingham stretching out on either side of the A612. The house was on a quiet, tree-lined street. It was not overlooked.

Physically Nic had led Ethan into the lounge, but psychologically Ethan had been leading the way from the first breath they had taken together. Ethan was feeling a level of freedom he had never experienced before. He had escaped from Darren's trap and had no doubt thrown Peter Jones's confidence seriously off kilter. As a consequence he was not only free to do as he liked, he was confusing his hunter at the same time. Soon he would be confusing and hurting his hunter. It wouldn't be long before he was damaging him permanently. And he hadn't even started with Marcus Kline yet.

Ethan looked at the room and breathed it in. He breathed in the atmosphere and the memories, the emotion and the expectation. In his experience, every home felt like a secure bubble, somehow connected to and yet safe from the world around it. In his experience that bubble was the thinnest of all protection, a falsehood, believed in by those who loved and needed so powerfully they couldn't accept how flimsy their sense of security really was. Ethan delighted in being in the homes of others, in breathing himself into them. He was doing that now as Nic invited him to sit in the floral-patterned armchair that faced the old-fashioned brick fireplace.

'I will stand if you don't mind,' Ethan said, gesturing towards the settee.

'Of course.' Nic sat. 'I know you, don't I?'

'Do you?'

'It feels like I do.'

'Do I look like someone you know?'

'Yes and no. It seems somehow as if I ought to know you, as if I really ought to, as if I've shared many things with you. It feels like that, but I can't quite make sense of it.'

'How does that make you feel?' Ethan wanted to giggle, but controlled himself.

'It's hard to put into words.'

'Then how does it look?'

'That's easier. It's as if I'm looking into a fog.'

'And where am I?'

'You're in the fog. Just. I can almost see you clearly but not quite.'

'We need to do something about that, don't you think?'

'Yes.'

'Good. I'm an expert at this sort of thing. I know exactly what you need to do. Just breathe in more deeply and deliberately and you will draw some of the fog in to you; that will make your vision clear, if only for a second. In that second you will recognise me.'

'OK.'

Nic did as he was told. Ethan watched, exhaling quietly and fully each time Nic inhaled.

'That's right. Take several more breaths. It might even help if you close your eyes.'

'Yes.'

Nic's eyes closed. Ethan continued breathing into him, penetrating on each inhalation, riding the breath, going deeper each time. 'You're nearly there,' he whispered.

'Yes.' Bright colours – red, gold and metallic blue – began to flicker around Nic's body as his heartbeat quickened.

Ethan let the heat build for a few more seconds before saying, 'Open your eyes. Now!'

Nic's eyes sprang open. His pupils were dilated fully, drawing in as much light as they possibly could, seeing every detail available to him, seeing more than he ever had before, seeing precisely what Ethan wanted him to.

'Andrew! Andrew is that really you?'

'Do you have to ask?' Ethan spread his arms, raising them to shoulder height, palms open, facing Nic.

'But…But it can't be!'

'Seeing is believing.' Ethan wiggled his fingers. He thought of worms wriggling and stretching out from palms nailed in place on a cross. He thought of them contracting and expanding as the body slumped. He thought of trillions of bugs in the gut changing in response to the physical stress, to the lack of oxygen, unaware that their host had just died. He wished he had been *that* centurion – if the story was true. After all, he could have created a religion if he'd wanted to. He just wasn't that cruel.

'Seeing is believing,' he said again. 'Who do you see, brother?'

'Oh my God! It is you!' Nic staggered. 'How can it be?'

'It's a miracle, a miracle of your own making. You've felt me close so many times. You've felt my touch. You've heard me whisper. The truth is you've stopped telling Peter because he doesn't believe and, just like all the others who lack your sensitivity, he mocks you. He believes it's a sign of your desperation and weakness. We know better. This is your reward. I'm here now.'

'Andrew…'

'Yes?'

'I've missed you so much. I've become so afraid.'

'Of what?'

'Of the possibility that Peter and the rest of them were right, that I was just imagining you, that your death really meant I had lost my older brother forever. I'd become so scared I was wrong.'

'And now?'

'Now I feel like a weight has lifted. Only it was a weight that was inside me and now I'm so open and so ready to welcome you back in where you belong. And so sorry I doubted you.'

'You don't need to be sorry for anything. You wanted to believe. They wanted to take it from you. Only they couldn't. They can't. Not now and not ever again. You have earned this. I'm here because of you, because of your love and your need. So take your openness and just welcome me in. More fully than ever before. And realise and remember I never left. And realise and remember I never will. I am your brother. Forever. We share more than you ever can with anyone else. Our relationship is unique. The car crash didn't kill my essence. The body you buried wasn't me. This is the real me. I am here for you. I am here now because I know how much you need me.'

Nic made no attempt to stop or wipe away his tears. His mouth hung open, incapable of sound, his head shaking from side to side with the silent disbelief of a person who had just won the world's greatest prize. Ethan lowered his arms slowly, drawing the raw emotion out of the other man; fuelling it with his every breath.

'You have no words. I understand.' Ethan smiled, letting his teeth show. 'The truth is, there are no words for what you are feeling and learning right now. So let me talk for both of us. I can see your pain and your turmoil. I can lead you to the decision you know is there, waiting for you to grasp it, the decision that will heal and strengthen you. Shall I take you there now? Shall we move on together? As brothers do.'

Nic forced the single word, 'Yes.'

'Good. It is time. We both know that to be true. It is time for you to free yourself, to become the man you truly are; the man you would already be if you had been loved properly. Your future is here now. You can feel it, can't you?' Ethan paused, watching Nic go even more inward. Then he continued. 'We are living in times of division and separation. The world is offering you its lesson. It is teaching you that it is right to break free, to seek your own destiny and be your own self. Anyone who would deny you that is your enemy. Anyone who says they love you and yet refuses to acknowledge this to be true is a selfish and hateful liar. It is time to break free from the herd, to rediscover your own beauty and worth.

'Now, as you listen to my words, as you feel them unlocking the fear that has held you captive for so long, you are beginning to see the distance that has existed between Peter and yourself for many years. A distance you have tried to bridge. A distance he created and maintained because you were not his true love. Instead you were his prisoner, trapped in a relationship of his making, one that suited his selfish needs and confined you to a position of inferiority.

'The reason why you feel so open right now is because you are seeing the distance between yourself and that hateful man growing ever greater. His hold over you is shrinking with every second. The belief that you needed him in your life is dissolving with it. Your unconscious now is erasing your ability to even remember his face. The colours and shapes are being smudged and changed, they are blurring as they diminish. When his face is gone from your memory, his voice will be next and, after that, so many other things about him will disappear comfortably and easily and only in the order that is best for you. This will continue for the rest of your life. Now, just take a moment, in silence, to let all of this settle and become true.'

As Nic sank ever deeper into the trance that was wiping his memories and changing his emotions, Ethan explored the atmosphere in the room and throughout the rest of the house. Just for fun he delved more deeply into the tension, the unfinished arguments and the silent pain that had been so obvious to him from the moment he had stepped inside. Then he went beyond, to what had once been the lightness and bright connectivity of hope and sharing and was now a dark blue background note. He willed it to shift further, to sink into the mud of life long since trampled.

Nic groaned softly. Ethan said, 'You have just realised haven't you? Using your real eyes you have seen safely that the relationship you once had with that hateful man was your version of a car crash, happening in slow motion, heading into inevitable destruction. Only now you are on a different journey. With me. To a very different place. A brighter, lighter place, filled with hope and new beginnings.' Ethan glanced at the photo on the white stone mantelpiece of Nic and his brother, Andrew, arms around each other, suntanned and smiling, their white shining teeth emphasised by the colour of their skin and the darkness of the night sky behind them. He had learned of Andrew's death from Calvin Brent, having requested information about all the individuals he planned to visit.

'What do you feel you must do now?' He asked.

'I must leave. With you.'

'Yes. Where must we go?'

'To somewhere bright, somewhere new.'

'How do you feel about doing this now?'

'Light. Hopeful. In ways I haven't been for years.'

'Good. Now, try hard and certainly in vain to remember who it is you are leaving.'

Nic breathed deeply. He frowned, shook his head. 'Someone, but I can't picture who.'

'Try harder.'

Nic tensed with the effort. 'The more I try, the more impossible it becomes. It's as if...' He cocked his head to one side and a smile almost formed as the question took shape. 'Was there actually ever anyone else?'

Ethan applauded. 'That's it! You see? Now you have realised the ultimate truth! There was no one else. Ever. It was just a dream. A dream you had a long time ago. In the real world there was only ever me. Me and you. And you will be able to remember me, see me, feel me, talk to me, always. All ways. Because we are connected in the most special way. Forever.'

'I know.'

'Of course you do. I am your proof. Here now.'

'I hear.'

'And?'

I can see it. And feel it.'

'So?'

'I have no time to waste. I have to leave immediately.'

'Yes! And make sure, too, that no one but me can ever contact you again.'

'Of course.' Nic took his mobile phone out of his jeans pocket and handed it over. 'This has everything and everyone. Without this I am completely free.'

'I will destroy it, as a symbol of your freedom. You will feel it happen. No one from this hateful place will ever contact you again. Now, go and pack a case. Take with you only the essential things you need. Leave behind everything that is in anyway connected to this prison. Take a bus into the city. Go to the train station. Look at the departures. One destination will stand out to you above all the others. Go to that place. To your destiny. I will already be there, having travelled in my own special way.'

'So we are doing this together?

'I will be around you at all times.'

'I need that.'

'I know.'

'Can I ask you one last thing?'

'Anything.'

'Will you help me if I … make any more mistakes with my life?'

'Be sure that I will protect you from the hateful people who might pretend they care for you. And, my brother, if all else fails I will help you realise what you have to do to become even closer to me. Remember, you were right all along, death isn't the end; it's just the best of new beginnings.'

'I will remember. Thank you.'

'Good. Now no more talking! Not here. Go! Pack! Leave! When you reach your new home give yourself time to settle in and then you will find me there. Now, let us both move!'

Nic turned and left the room. Ethan listened to his footsteps on the stairs. He heard a case being opened in a bedroom at the rear of the house and clothes being pulled from a wardrobe. He considered, not for the first time, whether or not he was taking the right course of action. He could, if he chose, kill Nic now and leave the body in the bedroom as a most special end-of-day present for Peter Jones. Perhaps that was more appropriate? One big, devastating hit rather than death by a thousand cuts? He heard more movement upstairs. Time was running out. What to do for the best?

As his mind raced, Ethan looked again at the photo of Nic and his brother. He was sure he could taste their scent coating his tongue. He resisted the temptation to spit. Somehow that act of will helped him make his decision.

He left the house several minutes later. As he strode through the carefully manicured front garden towards the Mercedes with its black tinted windows parked to the right of the gate, a quote from the Persian mystic and philosopher Epiah Khan flittered through his mind.

'The solidity of the edge is always next to the emptiness of the fall.'

The thought of Peter Jones and Marcus Kline falling into darkness they were as yet incapable of imagining made him almost giddy with excitement. One wrong step, one push, then fear leaping as the mind screamed and the body dropped into nothingness. Everything lost so quickly, with no chance of reversal, and no way of knowing when disfiguring, destructive impact would bring it all to an end.

Matt the driver started the engine as Ethan opened the passenger door and sat next to him. 'You look flushed,' he said.

This time Ethan made no attempt to stop himself giggling. The car had reached the end of the street before he was able to talk. 'I'm going to tell you something,' he said finally. 'Something the world doesn't know, something that's off the edge.'

'What?' Matt turned the Mercedes left onto the A612. The car in front signalled right and eased to a temporary stop before crossing the road into the driveway of a large, semi-detached house. Matt was grateful for the excuse to keep his eyes on the road.

'Crucifixion, 'Ethan said. 'It's too good for some people.'

34

Peter Jones didn't get home early. It was though, he reasoned, as early as he could possibly make it and that was all he had promised. He checked his watch as he walked from the car to the front door: 10.14pm. Early by his standards when working a major case.

But still not good enough.

Right now nothing he was doing seemed good enough. The way to turn it all around was to commit to the process and follow it, step by step; to learn from the feedback, adapt and move forward again. That, he reminded himself, was an integral part of the detecting process. And how he might save his relationship with Nic.

As he reached for his house keys Peter realised the house was in darkness. He stopped dead.

'Don't tell me you've gone to bed just to make a point!'

It was such a typical Nic ploy. So often he would stress the need for them to spend time together, or highlight a problem needing to be solved, and when Peter failed to meet the agreed timing he would postpone the conversation indefinitely. And then sulk and let it fester, pretending that it really hadn't mattered that much in the first place, turning it into a scene from the sort of 'B' movie he loved to teach about in his role as Lecturer in Film Studies at Nottingham Trent University.

'Shit!' Peter glared at the front door, giving himself a moment, forcing into submission the part of his psyche that was urging him to get back in the car and return to work. Whether Nic was asleep or just pretending to be, they were going to talk tonight. Peter had no idea what tomorrow would bring, but his best guess was that it would be more time-consuming trouble. He had to use the time available to him now to begin the process of reminding – and convincing – Nic that he loved him; that their relationship was worth fighting for.

He opened the door, locked it behind him, and turned on the hall light. It was obvious to him immediately. Something was different. Wrong. His policeman's instinct quivered. His hand reached instinctively for his phone, to call for back up. He stopped himself.

'Over-reacting,' he whispered. 'It is Nic after all.'

He switched on the landing light and walked upstairs loudly. The feeling grew. Peter was used to coming home to find Nic asleep. He knew what the house felt like when his partner was inside. He had long since become accustomed to the gentle underlying rhythm and pulse created when people shared a space. Only now their home didn't feel like that at all. It felt lifeless. Peter's breathing quickened as possibilities raced through his mind.

'Nic?' The shout left him uncontrolled; waking up his lover and having another furious row suddenly seemed the best of all options. 'Nic?'

Peter opened the bedroom door and turned the light on automatically. He gasped, reaching to the wall with his right hand as his usual strength drained out of him.

'Nic…' His eyes watered.

The bed was empty and unused. Nic's wardrobe was open and his clothes were missing. It was over. The evidence was overwhelming. Nic had gone. Their relationship was dead. His greatest fear had been realised.

Peter stared at the bed, at the dark blue duvet and the smooth white pillows. It looked now like a death mask; a perfect but empty representation of what once had been.

'Nic.' He said the name deliberately now, the last time

with love, a final farewell. He had no intention of chasing and searching him out, of trying to breathe new life into what had passed. All he could do from now on was process the pain quietly and focus on catching a killer. He knew all of that, even then, even as his body rocked and the agony of loss ripped through him.

He looked at his watch again. It was something to do. He didn't need to mark the time.

'Better late than never, eh? That's what they say.' He spoke to the empty bed as if it were a crime scene and the policeman in him smiled at the dark humour.

Better late than never.

Time for a drink, then.

He went downstairs, into the kitchen, and poured himself a large Balvenie 12-year-old, his favourite single malt. Nic hated the stuff. Peter downed it in one and poured himself another. There wouldn't be a leaving note. He was sure of that. Nic would have left in such a rush driven by a storm of emotion there would have been no time to write. Indeed, if he had tried he would have spent so long struggling to find the right words he would have talked himself into staying, at least for another day.

Peter drained the glass, reflected briefly on how quickly things empty out, and poured a larger measure. He looked out through the French doors into the garden at the rear of the house. It was a landscape that was easy to control, its hidden changes gradual and predictable.

If only it was all so easy.

'If it was all that easy, what the hell would I have done with my life? I depend on bad stuff bursting out without warning.' Peter took another large swallow of whisky.

Ethan Hall was out there somewhere, in his city, polluting it, damaging it. Left unchecked, his influence would burst out at some point and innocent people would be destroyed. Time was running out.

'Running out and running away. It seems to be the season for it. I stopped running years ago.' Another drink. No sense of its effect yet. He doubted it would touch him tonight.

At least, he reflected, Nic was now safe from Ethan's threat. That was the one good thing to come out of it all. The only thing.

The line flashed through his mind, daring him to sing it. He spat it out with forced humour, knowing it would hurt.

'Always look on the bright side of life...'

Peter fell asleep finally in the floral-patterned armchair in the lounge. He slept fitfully, his dreams a fearful, swirling mix of loss and failure and dread.

He woke early with a splitting headache and a sick feeling in his stomach to discover the United Kingdom had voted to leave the European Union.

PART 3

BELIEF

35

The edge is crumbling away.

Piece by tiny piece.

It's easy to miss the connectivity of it all, the inevitability of the complete collapse. Easy to treat each bit as if it is somehow separate from the rest. Easy to be so focussed on your own miniscule plot you forget that the fences you have created are false, and when one part falls it will pull the rest down with it.

Sooner or later every herd turns inward on itself. Members crash headlong, trample each other or throw themselves off the edge. Only this edge is crumbling, taking the ground away from beneath their feet whether they realise it or not.

The shift cannot be avoided. What I have begun – what I am going to do – is irreversible. And necessary. You have to destroy what is already in place in order to create something new. It takes insight and strength to know that destruction always leads – destruction and violence.

Sometimes violence creates a death, sometimes a birth. Either way something has to be ripped out. I want heart and soul. Influence always changes the inside first and I know how to penetrate.

You could not keep me out.

They have already failed to.

My words travel on the breath of my intention. Sometimes they are sharper than a knife, sometimes soft as the most gentle breeze. They breathe me in. I feel it. They carry me inside them. They process me. I change their brains and their bodies follow. I lead them to the edge. I turn them inward. I ensure destruction.

I am Shiva.

First. Last. Always.

36

Calvin Brent believed he was reading and managing the game with clarity and precision. As a gambler he knew the key to success was two-fold. Firstly, you had to identify probability accurately. Secondly, you had to know how and when to bluff brilliantly.

Some gamblers made the mistake of thinking that probability would morph into certainty. He knew better. He was a gambler and a gangster. And clever at both. As a result of his father's guidance, he knew how to learn from the experience of others rather than simply his own. He had seen too many gamblers and gangsters believe that, once the odds were stacked in their favour, a particular outcome was certain. They forgot the game wasn't over. And that nothing was certain until it had happened.

The game wasn't over yet with Ethan Hall. That meant nothing was certain. Even though the odds were stacked in his favour. Calvin Brent had factored in all the possibilities he could imagine and given what he knew about Ethan he had exercised his imagination as fully as he was able. Consequently, he had identified and covered or cut off options that ranged from the possible to the downright absurd.

'Better safe than sorry,' he told himself for the third time. 'Don't want to have to bluff with this one.'

The knock on his office door came right on cue: 9am. Everyone who worked for him knew he had a thing about punctuality. When he told you a time he demanded you meet it precisely. For him, a minute too early was as annoying as a minute too late. No one got it wrong twice.

'Matt, enter!'

The big man closed the door behind him and crossed the

floor in four, quick steps. He stood, as required, on the other side of his boss's desk, in precisely the same spot he always did. Brent noticed that he looked tired, as if the events of the day had been too much for him.

'Sit yourself down, take the weight off.'

'Er, OK. Thanks.'

Calvin enjoyed watching the mix of surprise and pride play on his employee's face. For his own part, he revealed nothing. 'Now, we have a couple of things we need to talk about. I want you to know I'm taking you into my trust over this,' he lied, 'you understand what that means, right?'

'Yes boss, of course. Absolutely.' Matt coughed, covering his mouth with a lightly clenched fist, shifting awkwardly in his chair.

'Good. As you've experienced first-hand this is a fucking unusual and potentially dangerous situation we find ourselves in. Ethan Hall has to be handled with care. Don't you agree?'

'He's a fuckin' freak an' a nut-job! Boss.' Matt shifted again.

'I didn't ask for a diagnosis, just for confirmation that you know how dangerous he is.'

'Sorry. Yes. He does stuff to people ya can't imagine.'

'That you can't imagine, Matt. Don't compare yourself to me.'

'No boss. Sorry.'

'And then to complicate things Darren fuckin' Smith, decided to sell him out. Which means he decided – actually made the conscious decision – to sell me out. Hall wasn't being protected by him, he was being protected by me. Just like he is now. That means when we've finished with Hall we need to have some communication with Smith. Right?'

'Absolutely. I can visit him last thing t'night if ya want me to.'

'No. I said, when we've finished with Hall!' Calvin sighed. 'Sequencing is everything, Matt. I don't expect you to understand that and to be fair you don't need to. Your work is all individual stuff, doing one thing at a time, dealing with specifics. It's what you're good at. That's why I keep you on. That and because I know you're loyal.'

'I'll do whatever you want, boss.'

'Exactly. So, before we talk about today let's take a moment to go back over the visits you made yesterday starting with the first one.'

'You wanna ask me abowt 'em again?'

'Why, have you got a problem with that?'

'No boss. Sorry.'

'Right. So tell me again, are you fucking sure the target was really fucked up when you left him?'

'Definite. He was fuckin' out of it. Unconscious covered in puke and shit.' Matt pulled a face.

'And there were no signs that Ethan had knocked him about in any way?'

'No. It looked just like he'd had some sort of heart attack or really bad reaction to something. It was like his insides had just had to come rushing owt, like e'd lost everythin'. He was grey even before we left. Wouldn't surprise me if he'd already died.'

'He won't have. Hall said he'd put him in a type of coma, that he'd need to go back to finish it. It didn't sound like he was bluffing. And I can't afford to take the risk.'

'Do you want me to go back and check?'

'No. I want as few visits as possible, limit the chance of some nosy fucking neighbour seeing something and talking about it later. So we'll concentrate on getting Ethan Hall around unseen today and leave coma-man until first thing tomorrow morning.'

'OK boss.'

Calvin watched the look of relief pass across the bald man's face. He'd never seen his enforcer this edgy and nervous before. He'd have thought that after Ethan Hall had made him put the gun in his mouth and almost shoot himself Matt would have been desperate to beat the shit out of the little fuck. Only instead he seemed keen to keep as far away as possible.

'If necessary, when you return, Hall will have to whisper a bit more in his ear and send him on his way fully.'

'Will you want me in the room?'

'Of course I fucking will. You're my eyes and ears. You'll make sure today goes according to plan, without attracting any undue attention, and tomorrow you'll make absolutely sure the person I want dead is stone cold.' Calvin scowled deliberately. 'You can manage one more day of this, can't you? I do need to know you can drive Hall around without pissing yourself.'

'Yeah. I'll be fine, no problem.' Matt coughed again. ''E's just really weird, ya know?'

'Before you know it, he'll be really dead.' Calvin smiled reassuringly. 'Tell me again what happened when you took him to Jones's place?'

'I dunno. Honest. I stayed in the car. He wa'n't in there too long. Came out looking like 'e was fuckin' royalty or somethin'. Started talkin' about crucifixion.'

'You didn't say that before.' Calvin tensed. 'You don't think he nailed the poor little bastard, do you?'

'No chance.'

'How can you be so sure?'

'There was no blood on him. And there would have bin. Christ, I've done less than that and bin covered in it.'

'Alright, but on either visit today if he comes out looking like he's creating a trail the coppers could follow, you let me know straight away. I don't expect him to get physical, that's obviously not his way, but you never know what might happen in the heat of the moment. So you keep your eyes open for even the slightest thing. I'll give you the first address when you leave here. Call me when he's done to ask for the second address. That'll be your chance to let me know if it's getting messy.'

'Gotcha.'

'When this is over I want it to seem like Ethan Hall has just disappeared. I want the cops to think he's got away somehow.'

'Only he won't 'ave.'

'No. Once everything's complete we'll go back to the original plan and Mr Hall will find out what happens to arrogant fucks who think they can tell me what to do.'

'Can I be there?'

'Of course. Once he's had his eyes taken out and his tongue cut off, I might even let you have a minute. A reward for doing a good job.'

'That would be fuckin' awesome!'

'I'm sure it would be.' Calvin grinned with the self-satisfaction of a job well done as his enforcer straightened in his chair, anger flashing in his eyes. 'I'm sure you've got plenty you'd like to share with him.'

'I'll break his fuckin' jaw!'

'Good man. Just keep that under control until we get to the very end. Clear?'

'Abso-fuckin'–lutely!'

'Excellent. And remember what I said, we save Darren until afterwards. Just think of it as normal, one job at a time.'

'I will. I'm on it, boss.' Matt hesitated briefly. 'Can I ask ya a question?'

'Why not?' Calvin sat back. 'I think today you're earning the right.'

'Ta. It's just that, I wondered 'ow ya knew t'get Hall out'a

Darren's place before the cops turned up.'

'Aah, that.' Calvin's mind flicked back automatically to the phone conversation when Ethan Hall had forced a change to the sequence of events, when he had also insisted he be moved to a safe house that Darren didn't know about. Calvin spoke without blinking. 'It's called reading the game, working out what's likely to happen and assessing the probability. It's what I do. It's what keeps me ahead of everyone else. I told Hall I was moving him out when he insisted on talking to me yesterday. He wanted to make some other changes, but for some reason he didn't want to do that. I had to insist. Make it clear who was running the show.'

Matt nodded, just too forcefully. 'I got it now.'

'Hmm. Well this,' Calvin scribbled an address on a piece of paper, 'is the next thing you need to have. That's where you're going first.' He handed it over. 'Burn it once you're done with it.'

''Course.'

'And, remember, make sure no one sees him.'

'Ya can count on it, boss.'

'I am. I'm counting on you to make sure everything works out as planned and that I don't see anything about this in the news. Now fuck off.'

37

Peter Jones couldn't believe what was in the morning papers. He had first seen the article over an hour ago and since then his disbelief and anger had only grown. When he arrived at Marcus and Anne-Marie's rented house, he was still clutching a copy of the morning edition.

Marcus opened the door. Peter flung the paper at his chest as he stormed past. He strode in to the kitchen where Anne-Marie was standing, holding a light blue mug in both hands. There was fear in her eyes. She looked paler more pale and fragile than the last time he had seen her. It didn't matter. He couldn't let himself care. There were too many lives at stake.

'What the fuck were you thinking?' He roared, turning back to face Marcus as he followed him in to the kitchen. 'Or were you not thinking at all? Were you just off on a Marcus-sized ego trip, desperate to claim back the spotlight you've clearly been missing for the last few months?'

'Are they the best questions you've got, Detective Inspector?' Marcus rolled the newspaper, opened the trash bin and dropped it inside. 'Is this how you skilfully manipulate people in your interview room, how you get them to confess before they even realise they've done it? Is this what they teach you at police influence school?'

'You selfish arrogant bastard! You're still so busy being Marcus Kline you can't see what you've done! That's the problem! That's always been the problem! When push has come to shove you've never been able to see past yourself.'

'As I recall I've seen far enough to have helped you on numerous occasions. And countless other people, too.' Marcus looked down as he spoke, tapping the fingertips of his right hand against the lid of the bin. His voice was rushed and cold. 'You can't do the work I've done all my life if you focus only on yourself. You have to know how to be fully attentive, how to forget who you are in order to recognise the reality of someone else. I wouldn't expect you to understand that. You just need to collect enough facts to make an arrest and get a conviction. Assuming, of course, you can stop the people you arrest from escaping.'

'No, no, no,' Peter shook his head, 'you're not drawing us away from the very real point at hand here. I'm not going to let you turn this into something it isn't. This is about your very deliberate decision to give an interview to a newspaper journalist, knowing full well and not caring about the fact that by doing so you were potentially jeopardizing any case we could create against Ethan Hall!'

'Jeopardizing! When you first caught him, you said the best you'd got for the three murders we know damn fine he committed was circumstantial! You said the only thing you could prove for sure was that it looked like he was going to kill me in the same way the others had died! You said in a court of law that didn't automatically mean he was the killer you'd been looking for, that you'd need to lead him into giving himself away when you eventually interviewed him – assuming, of course, that he lived. Well, he fucking lived all right, didn't he? And now he's out there somewhere. Close. He's close. I can feel him. And you've no fucking idea where. Or what he's doing. And you want me to sit back, stay here and do what – focus on writing a book? Pretend that everything will work out and that the good guys are going to win? Is that it? Eh? Is that really the best you've got?'

'We're not talking about the best I've got; we're talking about the almighty fuck-up you've created! Don't you understand that! You're right. Everything was a real fucking mess until this morning. If it were a game, Ethan would have been winning. But what you've just done isn't like scoring an own goal. It's like scoring a hat trick of own goals and then taking out your own goalkeeper!' Peter looked directly at Anne-Marie for the first time. 'Have you seen it?'

She shook her head.

'Did you know about it?'

She shook her head again.

'Beneath the heading "The challenge of being me" there's a detailed account of just what it feels like to be Marcus Kline right now. It's being pedalled as a unique and moving insight into what the world's greatest communicator is learning about himself as he goes through crisis.' Peter snorted and turned back to face Marcus. 'Believe it or not, this isn't just about you! There are lots of people involved in this, lots of people at risk, people we probably aren't even aware of yet. But you have to make it about yourself, don't you? And you have to go public with it no matter what the eventual consequence. Why? Because you're Marcus fucking Kline!'

'That's never been a problem to you before.'

'It's been a growing problem ever since Ethan Hall appeared on the scene!'

Peter paused to draw breath. Marcus looked again at the bin.

Anne-Marie asked in a quiet voice, 'Did you talk about us – about me – when you spoke to the reporter?'

The question made both men turn.

'No. Of course not. It was … a … a personal thing. I made sure of that. I was careful in what I said. I didn't … talk about anyone or anything else.'

'Why did you do it?' Anne-Marie's voice was barely more than a whisper.

'It wasn't planned.'

'So what are you saying,' Peter interjected, 'that you just happened to bump into a reporter on the street and decided there and then to give him an exclusive?'

'Yes. Actually. That's exactly how it was.'

'Yeah, right! Stop treating everyone like we're idiots, will you? Sooner or later there's going to be a conclusion to this, and my job is to make sure it's the right one! I'm going to do that no matter what shit you continue to throw in my way!'

'There's not much chance of that happening, when you can't recognise the truth when you hear it.'

'There's not much chance of it happening as quickly as it should when you keep forcing me to spend time dealing with your active disruption.'

'Police practice at its best – get minimal facts, lose emotional control, jump to a conclusion and waste time and energy getting everything completely wrong. No wonder crime is on the increase in this country. Our so-called best officers are severely lacking in analytical ability and emotional intelligence. What hope is there?'

'I have every fucking right to be angry! You have no ideas the prices we pay!'

'I thought your job was to care about everybody else and not yourself! I thought I was the selfish bastard?'

'If what you've done means our case breaks down I will – '

' – You'll what? Use me as your excuse for being incompetent?'

Peter's fists clenched.

'Stop it!' Anne-Marie shouted and stepped between them. 'Can't you see what you are doing to each other? Can't you feel the damage? How much more destruction do you both want? How much?'

Her outburst swamped their anger. Marcus pulled back,

shaking his head as if fighting tears. Peter relaxed his hands and exhaled slowly.

Marcus spoke first, 'I was just walking, trying to get my head together, trying to recreate some sort of inner control. I was struggling – failing miserably – to manage myself. I still am. No great revelation there, eh?' He half-smiled. 'The truth is I was on the edge of a breakdown. I'm sure I'm still there. Clinging on for dear life.

'Dave Johnson, the reporter, was hanging around near the office, hoping he'd see me. I didn't even see him coming. First thing I knew he was in front of me and I couldn't see a way past. I guess I just lost it. It felt like the only way I could avoid letting go and falling completely was to get angry and fight back. So I did. I gave Johnson a story thinking it would inflame Ethan, or at least draw him out and make him come after me. I figured if I faced him again, and was able to beat him this time it would be the quickest way to bring all this to an end. And, of course, create a foundation to start rebuilding myself from.' The half-smile returned. 'It sounds a load of bollocks when I say it out loud.'

'Words echo if we keep them inside for too long,' Peter said, 'new thoughts get lost behind their noise.'

'Good line!' Marcus nodded appreciatively. 'Where did that come from?'

'Your first book.' Peter chuckled. 'The fact you didn't recognise it really is a sign that your mind isn't where it normally is.'

'I can't argue with that.'

'So what happened to the silent internal state you always said was essential for influencing others appropriately?'

'Ethan Hall did.'

Peter reflected momentarily. 'Do you need to talk to a

professional?'

'I am a professional.'

'You can't talk to yourself.'

'Really? You should have heard some of the conversations I've had.'

As Anne-Marie listened to them she could feel the warmth returning, their friendship rekindling. 'Why didn't you talk to me about how you are feeling?' She asked.

Marcus looked up at the ceiling. 'How could I? We have other, far more important, things to talk about and do.'

'My health is not more important than yours.'

'It is to me. That's why I couldn't afford to let go, why I had to be strong.'

'We're a partnership. We help each other, that's the deal.'

'I know. It's just another of the things I've lost my way with.'

Anne Marie reached out and squeezed his hand. 'But what about Ethan?' She asked. 'Isn't there a real risk that he will respond how you thought and come after you again?'

'I think it's highly unlikely that Ethan will either want, or be able, to be that brazen,' Peter said before Marcus could reply. 'He's under a very different sort of pressure now, so I think you can relax on that front. And you know I'll do whatever I can to help both of you. But Marcus I do need you to keep out of the way. Just give yourself time to rest and recover. Do what you need to, between you, to look after each other. Leave Ethan Hall to me and my gang. Remember, as far as we know, he's done nothing to harm anyone since he escaped. Remember, too, that he's a novice at hiding and he's sure he can't be beaten, so he's bound to make mistakes. That means we are bound to catch him.'

'Fingers crossed.' Marcus made the gesture. 'What prices?' He asked suddenly.

'What are you talking about?'

'You said I have no idea about the prices you pay. What prices were you talking about?'

'Oh. Nothing specific,' Peter licked his lips, 'the tension, the late hours, the usual police stuff. Nothing that gets in the way of us doing our best work.'

Anne-Marie put her hand on his forearm. 'You look after yourself, too. Make sure you keep you and Nic safe just as you are the rest of us.'

Peter nodded. 'I need to go,' he said. 'I've got lots to do. I'll see myself out.' He turned and left.

After the briefest silence in which they both considered different things Marcus said, 'I am strong enough to keep working with you, you know that right?'

'As long as you are sure. If we have to take a break for a few days I doubt it will make any difference.'

'We don't need to take a break.'

'In that case, I need you to tell me what you are going to do to look after yourself.'

'Walk,' Marcus said, 'I'm going to walk myself back into my best ever form.'

'In the valley?'

'In the city. I need the hustle and bustle. It will provide the measure for how well I'm progressing.'

'You'd better get walking then.'

'I better had.'

38

Liam Hemsall had taken to spending time in the countryside. Every morning between 10am and 12pm he drove out along the A614 to Darcliff Wood some nine miles north of Nottingham city centre. He parked his car, a silver grey Vauxhall Astra, and walked alone, following the same pathways, trying to find something new every day.

It was proving to be his most personal therapy; a time for reflection in a place that reminded him of nature's inevitable change, its cycle of life, death and rebirth. Liam hoped it would eventually encourage him to look at things with a new perspective, to find new insights and learning, to silence the unwelcome voice that kept filling the space in his mind with its constant, *'Pull, pull, pull...'*

This morning he had watched a squirrel scurrying and searching. It had occurred to him the squirrel was a perfect example of its kind, that in one sense all squirrels were. 'So busy just being what you are, there's no space for questions and doubts and what ifs,' he murmured. The squirrel stopped when it heard his voice. It half-turned and looked up. Liam was sure he could see his reflection in its big, round eyes. The squirrel gave him only a few seconds and then set off again.

Now, as Liam walked he couldn't help but wonder what life would be like without the fears and challenges of being human.

'It would be boring.'

The voice startled him. He spun in its direction. His eyes met those of Ethan Hall. They drew him in.

'We are the top of the food chain,' Ethan said, 'and that brings with it unusual pressures and obligations. As a counterbalance though we do have the ability to make up our own minds, weigh up the pros and cons of any given situation, and then take the best way out. Who'd be a squirrel at the mercy of its environment when you can be like us, holding the power of life and death in our own two hands? Would you truly change places?'

'I … I don't know.'

'Yes, you do. Deep inside you know the answer precisely. You've just been scared to bring it to the surface. If you don't believe me just let yourself drift inward, see what you find. It's a very warm, safe place. Go on, give yourself permission.'

Somewhere in the back of his brain Liam sensed an alarm. It became an increasingly distant warning, disappearing as what felt like the most comfortable blanket descended gently over his conscious mind. He couldn't stop looking at Ethan. He couldn't prevent himself from easing into a state he had never felt before. Time reversed.

Suddenly he was a child again, safe in his own bed, knowing he needed to get up and face the day but far too cosy to make the effort, choosing instead to snuggle even deeper.

'Mmmm.'

There was no better place, nowhere more secure.

'I love it here,' he said.

'Of course you do,' Ethan replied. 'And the more you let yourself breathe naturally, the more that place will surround you and protect you. Just listen to my words now and they will lead you back to where you most need to be. And this is only the beginning, Liam. Just imagine a bed that goes on forever. A bed that is the keeper of your most private dreams and hopes and thoughts. A bed that is deeper than the warmest, softest ocean, that draws you down into its absolute promise with every passing second. A bed that is yours and your alone. There with you always. Your special home within your home. Surrounding you now as you breathe and listen and feel how your unconscious knows this so very well and everything is just a dream and every dream just draws you in deeper and deeper and…'

Ethan let his voice fade away as he walked to within one pace of Liam. He reached out and placed his gloved hands on Liam's shoulders, exerting pressure.

'Now you can truly feel the weight you are carrying, the burden pressing you down, inside and out. You carry it with you wherever you walk. It makes your footprints deeper. It hurts you and the ground beneath you. It is a weight you will carry for as long as your feet tread this earth. Unbearable. Inescapable, because we are born to move on the planet, born to move with our past always present, weighing us down.

'Now Liam you don't have to wait anymore for a resolution. You are feeling already the only safe place wrapping around you offering more beautiful dreams than you can ever…know as you hear me here, the only way to free yourself from the weight is to end the waiting, looking up to the heavens now for their support, getting ready to take your heavy, bruising feet off the sacred floor of this earth, getting ready to break the chain you have created and fly into your dreams…Make sense, Liam.'

'Mmmm.'

'And it feels right and good now, does it not?'

'Mmmm.'

'Good. Now stop looking heavenward and look at me instead.'

Liam did.

'I want you to realise in this dream you can still say words and people will hear you and you will hear yourself and you can remember things and you will feel the way the remembering makes you feel, and the more real it sounds and the more real it feels the more dreamlike it really is. Do you understand?'

'Yes.'

'Good. Because we are sharing this hear now as I help you remember some bright and vivid happenings and feel fully the feelings inside, and as you do these things notice your unconscious urging you to pull yourself free from this earth you damage. Because every little boy wants to fly in his own magic bed and every broken man yearns for the pull of redemption.

'So watch now as the images appear, quickly one after the other and, no matter how fast they come you will see them all as if you are back in that place and time, reliving each as if you are truly there, seeing it as if it is happening all around you, feeling the pull, pull, pull of the past from which you have to – and will soon – escape. Are you ready?'

'Yes.'

'Good. Eyes wide now.'

Ethan spoke for the next five minutes without stopping, using his words to create irresistible images – films – in Liam's mind. He took him back to their violent meeting in Marcus's home. He talked of the sound and feel of the bullets entering his chest, of how badly Liam's psyche had been affected. He talked of how much he, Ethan, had learnt and travelled and escaped in the safety of his hospital bed. Then he led Liam back once again to childhood memories of his own bed, contrasting that with the fear and sense of failure currently burdening him. He described the suffering that had happened and was still to happen because of Liam's inability to kill him. He took Liam's feeling of self-guilt and made the weight of it heavier than it had ever been. And then he tapped both of Liam's shoulders with the palms of his hands and by doing so he doubled the pressure. And then he did it again. And all the while he talked in his own special way, using his words to create images and feelings from which there could be no escape.

He talked like that until Liam was on his knees, sobbing uncontrollably. And then he said, as if they were sharing a gentle conversation during a mid-morning stroll, 'We are next to Tithe Green Burial Ground. Do you know that? Actually, I'm sure you do. I understand you have been walking here daily.' He smiled and went on, 'you can have your ashes buried with a tree of your choice planted on top. I know because for a while, many years ago, I planted trees here. It's a place to put down roots, is it not?'

'Yes.'

'So what do you need to do now?'

'Be alone.'

'And?'

'Escape.'

'From?'

'The pull of it all.'

'The pull is also the solution, the way out of this and into endless dreams. A flight back into childhood.'

'I know.'

For the first time since he had made his presence known Ethan turned his back on Liam and retrieved the two items he had laid on the ground. 'Here', he said, 'these are my gifts for you, to help you sleep.'

He offered both, one in each hand. Liam forced himself to his feet and took them eagerly. A sturdy, wooden three step ladder and a four metre length of three strand manila garden rope.

'These will stop you hurting the earth,' Ethan said. 'The waiting's over.'

'Thank you.'

'Believe me, it is my pleasure.' Ethan gestured towards a tree with a branch stretching solid and strong a couple of metres above the woodland floor. 'Now, let me watch.'

39

The synesthete leant back against the nearest tree trunk, folding his arms and tilting his head to one side, as Liam prepared his death.

He began by throwing the rope over the branch Ethan had indicated. Positioning the ladder beneath it, Liam stepped up and knotted the rope securely in place. He jumped back to the ground, grabbed the rope and pulled on it twice. The rope tightened its grip. The branch held firm.

Next Liam tied a simple running bowline knot, creating a noose. He tested that, too, nodding in satisfaction. At no point did he look again at Ethan Hall, or at the woodland or at the sky.

Holding the rope in his right hand, Liam stepped back onto the ladder. He placed the noose over his head with the knot on his left side. He pushed the rope as low as it would go. Then he tightened the knot.

Ethan observed how calm and deliberate the policeman's movements were. Despite that, the colours emanating from him were starting to change as the survival instinct tried to fight its way through the trance Ethan had created. Spikes of dark red began to appear – anger and urgency – flashing into the more tranquil mix of blues and gold. Occasionally an individual spike threatened to spread out, like flood water breaching a defence, but the state held firm and Ethan supported it, matching his own breathing to Liam's, controlling his heart rate, calming his central nervous system. The spikes subdued. Ethan returned to watching the more obvious activity.

Liam checked the knot one last time. He let his arms hang by his sides. He moved his feet forward slightly, to the very edge of the step. He bent his knees. He turned his head left, then right. The course rope scored his neck. He dropped his chin. He raised his hands, looked at them briefly and then put them in his trouser pockets. He took a deep breath. Held it. Closed his eyes. And kicked the ladder away.

Liam Hemsall had attended the scenes of several suicides by hanging. He knew how it worked. So-called short drop hanging killed in one of two ways. Either by cutting off the oxygen supply to the brain, or by compression of the arteries and veins in the neck. Or, of course, it could do both. He knew, too, that the vast majority of such suicides were achieved by tying the knot on the left side of the neck, constricting the jugular vein, preventing blood from getting back to the heart. It took less than 5lbs of pressure to constrict the jugular. It really didn't require much of a drop at all. In fact, if the rope was tied correctly you could hang yourself whilst kneeling on the ground.

As he stood on the ladder, feeling the rope against his skin, Liam found himself becoming unbelievably calm. And warm. And cosy. *Maybe Heaven's just the best dream of all,* he thought as he pulled the knot even tighter.

He let his arms relax and felt his feet move forward instinctively. He had been told dying in this way was often very painful. That no matter how committed the person was, their body inevitably thrashed, desperate for air, fighting against the compression of the noose and the weight of their body supported entirely by their neck and jaw. He knew it could take up to three minutes for unconsciousness to set in. He knew the body could live for many more minutes after that.

For a reason that he didn't understand at all, Liam felt the urge to turn his head from side to side. Doing so he could feel the roughness of the hemp against his skin. There was something strangely reassuring about it.

He raised his palms. They were the last things he wanted to see. The lines were obvious and varied, an intricate pattern, deeper than he had ever noticed, a work in progress. That, he remembered, is what the psychologist had said in answer to his question, 'Who am I?'

A work in progress.

Indeed this was. Just like everything else.

Time to sleep.

Liam realized that his hands were no longer in front of his face; they were in his pockets. Clearly everything was ready. Just one more thing to do.

Liam stepped forwards and kicked the ladder behind him.

Reality hit.

The tree groaned. He tried to gasp. Too late. The pain was worse than anything he could have imagined. His feet kicked. His hands grasped. The rope bit. His eyes felt like they were going to explode. His body twisted, jerked and fought its way to death.

The last thing Liam thought he saw before he lost consciousness was a squirrel looking up at him.

40

Anne-Marie Wells was lost in thought. She was looking at a range of images. They were photos she had taken of the storage unit in which most of her and Marcus's furniture and larger personal belongings were being kept.

Until yesterday she had made a point of staying away from the unit and all it contained. Her phone conversation with Peter, though, had shifted her perspective and with it her thinking. She had subsequently spent over an hour taking pictures from every conceivable angle, pictures of the unit in its entirety, of the way different objects had been stored; how they were juxtaposed against each other. She had taken pictures of boxes, the corners of boxes, and different wrapping, of the ceiling, the floor and of shadows.

When she and Marcus had decided to move out of their real home, they had talked long and hard about what to do with their possessions. She had wanted to take everything with them, keep it all together, do the best they could to recreate the sense of home they had shared for so many years. Marcus had argued against that. He had said they needed to rent a furnished property, to take with them only the essentials. Doing anything else, he reasoned, would be inviting the past to bleed into the present and, on a personal level, he needed space, a clean break from all-too-easy reminders of how Ethan Hall had invaded their world. Anne-Marie had agreed reluctantly.

As her illness worsened the urge to visit the unit had grown. She hadn't understood why and she had resisted it until yesterday. Then realization had dawned. It felt like an almighty release.

A storage unit was, in essence, a characterless, clean box, even though some companies chose to call them *rooms*. Units varied in size, anything from twenty square feet upwards. If you had the need there were units in which you could store your entire life.

They were places you turned to only when you were making a change or requiring secrecy. No matter how long you used the unit for, the relationship was essentially transitory. You never owned the unit, only what you chose to put in it. And when you moved out, someone else moved right in.

Anne-Marie's realization felt like it had exploded inside her, casting one insight after another into her consciousness. First of all, she had been wrong to want to move everything with them. Having all of your belongings in one place didn't turn that place into your home. No, a home was something altogether different; a creation independent of the objects it contained. The house they were staying in now could never be their home, but that wasn't because their furniture was missing. It was because they had been forced here. And one day, they – Anne-Marie checked herself – *Marcus* would move on to find and build a new home.

Secondly, even a home was transitory. The house they called home had been built fifty years before they bought it. Two other families had called it home before they did. And now someone else was filling the same space, creating their own, unique version, believing they owned it. In one sense, the buildings marketed as homes were just a form of storage unit. Albeit a unit you could fill with emotion.

Thirdly, whilst most people bought their home because of location, or kerb appeal, or the number of rooms, the most important thing a real home provided was space. Space to grow and learn and share in response to life's changes. That night, over ten years ago, when she and Marcus had promised each other *for better or worse* that's precisely what they were talking about. A commitment to sharing the space they called life and all the caring, creativity, challenges, clutter and chaos that might come their way.

Sitting on the uncomfortable settee, looking down at the several dozen photos she had laid out on the floor, Anne-Marie shifted uncomfortably. She patted her stomach.

'Just a storage unit,' she whispered, standing upright for the first time in half an hour. She pulled her ribcage upwards and out, stretching her stomach, seeking to ease the tension. The next time she looked at the photos she found herself concentrating on the space between them, the space around and above them. It was a technique for gaining new perspectives she had learnt many years ago as a fledgling photographer. At that time she had been reading lots about Buddhism. She had even done a little meditation. It was a practice she had secretly started again.

Anne-Marie let herself become aware of the way the objects in the room, including the photos, fitted into the space, trying to see the actual space rather than anything else. It was a way of looking she had forgotten about until just now.

'We are never taught to look at the space,' she reminded herself, 'only at the objects. And if we try to see space, we can't. We acknowledge space only because of the absence of things. Yet space came first. It's the biggest of everything there is. You can't have storage if there isn't space.'

Peter's suggestion that if she had to do a photo about the inevitability of her death she should title it *Processing* had unlocked her subconscious. Her subsequent realisations had led to a simple and powerful conclusion. The photo could only be set in the storage unit. It made perfect sense. She didn't know either the structure or detail yet, but the setting was fixed. As was the title: *Space*.

One of her favourite Buddhist quotes read, 'Silence is an empty space, space is the home of the awakened mind.' Her mind felt fully awake. The final photo in her last ever collection would encapsulate everything she had come to realize about storage and space and the inevitability of change.

As Anne-Marie tried to relax and stretch and see the invisible, she heard the front door open and close. She looked at her watch. He was back earlier than expected.

'How was the walk?' She asked, stepping into the hall to greet him.

'I didn't walk,' Ethan Hall said. 'I have my own taxi.'

Anne-Marie screamed.

41

Peter Jones was missing something. He knew it. There was something there, somewhere, that he couldn't quite see or grasp and he needed to.

'So what the hell is it?'

'Sorry, boss?' Kevin McNeill looked up from the paperwork he was reading.

'Talking to myself,' Peter admitted. 'But if it's a good enough question to ask myself, it's good enough to ask you. We're missing something – a detail, a connection – some factor we ought to be able to recognize or predict. So the question is, what is it?'

Kevin pondered. 'Maybe Ethan Hall has a second friend. Maybe he moved in with them when he got spooked at Smith's?'

Peter shook his head. 'We've been through Hall's history too thoroughly for that to be the case.'

'Then maybe Hall's more equipped to avoid us than we give him credit for? After all, he kept himself under the radar for years before he went after Marcus. We have always assumed he wasn't up to anything during that time, but the truth is we've got no idea what he might have done. He could be responsible for all sorts of stuff. Let's face it, there's more we don't know about him than we do.'

'True. To me, though, it just doesn't feel as if there's a gap we have to fill; it's more like an obviousness we're missing.'

'That's your stomach talking?'

'Yep.'

Can't you just burp up the answer?'

'Very funny.'

'I thought it was a gas.'

Peter smiled grudgingly. 'Thinking of a new career in comedy are we, Detective Sergeant?'

'Absolutely not, boss.'

'Don't blame you. Now, back to the question at hand. Tell me again everything we know about Ethan Hall and his recent activity.'

Kevin sat back in his chair and looked up at the ceiling. 'He walked out of the hospital having seriously messed with a young Constable's head. He went to stay with a man he knew from some time before – we can call him a friend, but I really don't think Ethan has any friends –'

'– Stick to facts,' Peter ordered.

'The fact is we know he left Smith's at about the same time we were told he was there. The fact is someone has to have seen him since then. The fact is he has to be staying somewhere. The fact is we haven't got a clue where.'

Peter shook his head a second time. 'No. Let's keep believing that we've got the clue and we're just not recognising it.'

'That's not like us.'

'We can't do perfect.'

'And we don't need to, to be the best.' Kevin completed his DCI's well-known phrase.

'Precisely. So we can't let ourselves be blinded just because Ethan Hall is so out of the ordinary. We have to keep reminding ourselves and the rest of the team of the context. Ethan Hall is a criminal and we are professional criminal catchers. He is playing our game not vice versa. Keep pumping that message.'

'Will do.'

Peter's mobile phone rang. The news tore through him like a knife. 'Fuck! Fuck! Fuck!'

Kevin stood automatically. 'What is it?'

'Liam Hemsall was found hanged less than an hour ago. All

the indications are it's a suicide.'

'Dear Christ!' Kevin slumped. 'Where?'

'Not at home. Woodland.'

'Small blessings.'

'Small and significant. Someone is with his family now.' Peter thought back to the night of Ethan Hall's arrest; the night PC Liam Hemsall had pulled his gun and fired in defence of himself, a colleague and a member of the public; the night they all thought had marked an ending.

'Have you ever had to shoot anyone, boss?' Kevin's question interrupted his reflection.

'No. Had to draw my gun a couple of times, back in the day, in a different role.'

'Could you have pulled the trigger?'

'Yes.'

'Because of the training?'

'Because if you care enough to carry a gun, you should care enough to be willing to fire it.'

'As Liam did.'

'Yes.' Peter felt the pain and anger twist and tear at his stomach. He surrendered to the sensation, having learnt from bitter experience it was better to focus on the physical feeling rather than the associated narrative. Most people tried to escape the pain of loss, or regret or failure, not realizing the only way to do so was by jumping into and reinforcing an all too often destructive story they had been carrying deep inside themselves for many years. So instead, Peter chose to focus on the pain.

He couldn't help, though, but think of Nic. Some part of him wanted to say *Just another in a long line of relationship fuck-ups!* but he silenced the voice and observed instead the cold feeling that was already beginning to settle in. He wasn't sure when it had started, but he could feel it now and he was going to do nothing to reverse it. The emotion he had once felt for Nic would freeze – painfully at first, the way ice always burnt – and he intended to let it grow until it was as hard and dense as rock.

'How many different pains can one person carry?' He asked without meaning to.

'Boss?'

'Nothing.' Peter's heart quickened suddenly. 'Say it again!'

'What exactly?'

'That bit about the facts of Ethan Hall.'

'I, er, I said that someone had to have seen him since he left Darren Smith's, and that he had to be staying somewhere.'

'Exactly!' Peter thumped his right fist into his open palm. 'Someone has to be helping him. Someone has to have seen him and yet no one has told us they have, even though there is a sizeable reward on offer. How do you explain that?'

Kevin shrugged. 'Perhaps he's just been lucky?'

'Or perhaps he's got professional help? Think about it. How does an amateur working alone beat a team of experienced professionals? Answer – they are either lucky as you suggest, or they get the very best of professional support. Now, who could provide such help for Ethan?'

'Calvin Brent!'

'And who does Darren Smith work for ultimately?'

'Calvin Brent!'

'So what if Darren Smith told Calvin that not only was he mates with Ethan, he was also putting him up?'

'And what if Calvin then decided he wanted to meet the new, freaky villain on his block?'

'Of if Ethan demanded to see him?'

'Jesus!' Kevin paused for breath. 'If Ethan Hall and Calvin Brent joined forces, we'd be in for all sorts of trouble.'

'We would be,' Peter said, 'only I don't think any form of

long-term collaboration between the two is likely.'

'Why not?'

'Because they are both power freaks. The best they could manage is a short-term, mutually beneficial trade-off.'

'OK. So Calvin Brent could keep Ethan safe, but what could Ethan do for him?'

Peter gestured upwards. 'Any fucking thing he asked him to. It's a perfect one night stand.'

'So what happens afterwards?'

'Calvin brings it to an end in his own unique fashion.'

'You mean he kills Ethan?'

'What else would he do?' It was Peter's turn to shrug.

'So why don't we just leave them to it?'

'Because we are the police!' Peter slammed his hand onto Kevin's desk. 'Remember?'

'Hadn't forgotten, boss.'

'It would be a serious mistake if you ever did! Now, let's get to doing what we do best. Let's work on the premise that Calvin Brent is using and protecting Ethan, and that Ethan is using Calvin.'

'Which means that Calvin has put Ethan into one of his safe houses.'

'Indeed it does. And given that we are aware of several of those houses, we can get eyes on them straight away.'

'And what about the ones we're not aware of?'

'We need to get them identified asap! Let's ramp up the pressure and the incentives. Squeeze everyone we know! This is our best chance of finding Ethan Hall, so let's treat it as such.'

Peter watched a grim look of determination spread across Kevin's face. 'I just want to stop him before he destroys another life!' He said.

Peter nodded. His gut tightened. 'Let's hope we can.'

42

It seemed to Anne-Marie that her scream echoed in the hall. She could see Ethan talking to her, but couldn't hear a word he was saying. She could feel his eyes boring into her, but couldn't look away. She wanted to run, but was rooted to the spot.

Finally the echo faded.

'I'm here to help you,' Ethan was saying. 'Whatever you might think, whatever they've told you about me, I've done much good. I've helped lots of people in my time; enabled them to make the most positive changes at the most critical moments in their lives. That's why I'm here now, why I've come to see you before I move on for good. I've come to do what only I can.'

Ethan began walking towards Anne-Marie. Just when she was sure he was going to touch her, he turned left into the lounge. 'Follow me please,' he said. 'It will be more comfortable in here. And it is time you had some comfort back in your life, wouldn't you say?'

'Yes.' The answer escaped before she realised it. Her feet were following him, too.

Ethan walked over to the bay window. He was silent for a moment as he took in the view. 'The valley is beautiful,' he said, keeping his back to her. 'You must adore it.'

'Yes.'

Ethan turned. His smile made her think of the most innocent child. 'I love nature,' he said. 'It's where I've worked most of my life.' It seemed to Anne-Marie that he was blushing slightly. 'Although, of course, you might know that. I'm guessing you've heard lots of stories about me. I'm sorry for some of them. And I'm sorry we met the way we did. This meeting is going to be very different, I promise. Please, sit.' He gestured towards the settee.

Anne-Marie sat. There was a softness about him, a steady, persuasive energy, like the warmest and softest of currents. The settee had never felt so comfortable.

'Now, let's begin.' Ethan sat too, in the armchair facing her. 'One of the prevailing stories you will know is that I am able to influence people profoundly. It's a gift I was born with and have worked to develop. I'm going to use it today to help you. Is that OK?'

Anne-Marie nodded.

Ethan smiled again. 'You have questions,' he said. 'I can see their colour. You can be relaxed, you are safe and you can ask me anything you want. Two questions only, though, for obvious reasons I can't stay with you indefinitely.'

Anne-Marie knew the first question instantly. 'Why?' She asked.

'Why have I come here to help you?'

'Yes.'

'Because this whole thing can only end badly for me. I'm not stupid – far from it – so I know the truth of this. And many people will believe it's what I deserve. It shouldn't, though, end badly for you. And everyone knows you don't deserve it to. So I'm going to make the difference on your behalf. In a moment, when we stop talking like this, you are going to feel your state deepen and change. Let me say again, you will be completely safe throughout. In fact, you will love it. And that will be the start of you returning to complete health.'

'But Marcus – '

' – Has been trying. I understand that. He knows, too, as you do, that he has been failing. Without me, the consequence of his failure is your death.' Ethan looked at the photos on the floor. He had walked over them without disturbing their order. 'Because of me, you will be able to plan and share a different photo story.'

'How can you be so sure?'

'I work with nature, remember?' The smile returned. 'I don't think that was the second question you had planned, was it? I think you've just snuck an extra one in.'

'Yes.' Anne-Marie almost giggled. 'Can I still ask another?'

'Why not? It is quite literally the least I can do for you. So, fire away.'

'Why were you going to kill Marcus?'

'To be honest with you, that's just a personal thing. A mixture of an experiment and a lesson. It has nothing to do with you and me.'

'He's my husband!'

'I was talking to your cancer, not the rest of you.'

Anne-Marie gasped. Her body trembled.

'Best of all,' Ethan continued, 'this will be our secret. You are going to get better and you can let Marcus believe he was responsible. That will give him everything he needs to help him recover from the realisation that he isn't the world's greatest. You see, between us we will now solve both of your problems. You will have the most powerful healing experience. Your husband will be spared a complete, irreversible, breakdown and his career will grow again. The two of you will have a future you can look forward to.'

Anne-Marie couldn't believe what she was hearing, and yet it felt real and true in every fibre of her being. She risked another question. 'Can I really trust you?'

'Feeling is believing.' Ethan leaned forwards. 'And it's time for you to feel.' He blinked once. Anne-Marie's eye closed and her head dropped forwards. Ethan reminded himself of his intention and then eased his awareness even further back than it already was.

He felt his brain stem, then travelled down his spine into his coccyx and stretched that with a gentle exhalation. Then he moved back again, into the space beyond his physical self, where clarity shone.

He spoke without thought or planning, as he always did from this place. 'Anne-Marie, you know my voice now. And my voice will play in your mind forever. You will hear and feel it in so many healing ways, knowing change is everything and all there is, and the only thing one should fixate on is the truth that everything changes, so there is nothing to fix or heal, there is neither right nor wrong, there is just breath and loss, and we can lose anything because we are only change and so there is nothing to hold on to, and so there is nothing to lose, because...

'Just breath this understanding into your unconscious. In. And out. And keep doing so forever, because numbers are a human construct only. Nature teaches instead to move through and in and out and on...and on...Nature cannot be counted. Can you? Now? Changing because this is your true nature, without labels or expectations or even...anything...else. Only the air of the universe, in and out, cycling, changing, moving on...and on...and on...into the space that is everything inside and out...breathing in from space into space, making space for change and newness and well-being as you are already using your unconscious now to open to this new life, because your response-ability is here, now, being change and space-full and...'

Ethan Hall watched as Anne-Marie sank into the deepest of trances. He left her there and looked again at the valley, noticing how different it seemed from his new, more distanced, perspective. He sat unmoving, barely breathing, for fifteen minutes. Then he said, 'Very slowly now, and only in your own time, let your breathing begin to move higher up into your chest, and as it does so will your awareness rise with it, and as it does so will you change, knowing change always happens on the inside first at the rate and speed at which you feel most comfortable. And when you open your eyes, you will realize how much colour there is in the world, and one of those colours – only you will know which, it might be gold, it might be green, it might be… will make itself known to you in new, positive ways, reminding you sometimes consciously and always sub-consciously of the healing that is happening always, with every breath, whether sleeping or awake, because if we can create something we can obviously create something new in its place, in one way or another, just as a mirror holds nothing permanently and shows only what is present briefly. Reflecting on this, whenever you are ready, light up, give yourself permission to go forwards, moving again into a bright, new shining world.'

Anne-Marie felt as if she was floating up from the ocean bed. It was a most peaceful, joyous journey. She experienced the movement in a way she never had before; so connected to each subtle shift that time appeared to have stopped and her fear of death – the cause of it – disappeared.

When she surfaced and opened her eyes, Anne-Marie reeled with the intensity of what she saw. Everything seemed brighter. Even the carpet and the dull, worn furniture. Even the ceiling. And the sky and the valley beneath shone with a promise it could barely contain. She couldn't help but wonder why, as a photographer, she had never seen it before.

'It's so beautiful!'

'What exactly?'

'All of it. The colours – especially the greens – and the connections, the way it all fits together so perfectly.'

'And?'

'I feel a part of it. I feel as if I'm looking at myself. Only that doesn't really make sense because I'm not sure I have a self in the way I used to think I had. It's really weird, really lovely. I'm looking at the grass, seeing it stretching out, covering, moving so subtly, growing out of the earth, drawing in from the sky, so humble and vibrant and essential.'

'The grass connects with you,' Ethan lowered his inflexion, creating a statement rather than a question.

'Yes. Or maybe I connect with it. Or maybe that sort of division is completely false.'

'We are all just a part of nature.'

'I know.' Something in Ethan's voice and in what he said reminded Anne-Marie of Marcus. The association made her stomach flutter. Suddenly everything felt different.

'Right now,' Ethan said, 'knowing is the least important of all things. And being is the most...and breathing, in and out. Now hear. Nowhere is the place to bed down in this current... situation...shining and sinking...colourful and safe...breathing and sinking...lifelong...deeper and deeper.'

Because Ethan had not let Anne-Marie fully out of the first trance, she fell into the second one more quickly and completely. He watched her body change as the state took her and drew her in. He enjoyed the way her consciousness surrendered willingly and completely. He drifted back again, beyond himself, and continued to talk. He knew her cancer was no match for him.

Sometimes Anne-Marie thought she could hear Ethan's words and when she did she felt she was taking them in like food, resting on them as if they were a pillow, moving through them as if they were a field of long grass. Sometimes she was aware only of her complete lack of awareness, observing her own state from some previously unknown distant place. Sometimes she lost every sense of her own existence.

Ethan Hall saw it all. His connection with her was absolute. He knew she would forever be drawn to the valley, to the feel of the grass beneath her feet and its colour all around her. 'It will be your lover,' he whispered, realising as he heard the words that it was time to lead Anne-Marie back.

It took several minutes before she was able to talk and look and move as she usually did. When she could, her fear returned.

'What happened?'

'Change. Profound, personal, intimate change. We shared it together.'

Anne-Marie shivered.

'It's for the best. Remember. This way we all win.'

'How do you...?"

'I win because I'm pleased to save you.'

'Is that all?'

Ethan smiled. 'Time now for us both to move.' He stood up. 'Come.'

Anne-Marie followed him back into the hall. She couldn't help but notice how the light of the day shone through the glass panel in the front door. She tried instinctively to move past Ethan towards it. He stopped her, his left hand grasping her right forearm.

'Not yet,' he said. 'First, you have to show me your bedroom.'

43

Ethan kept hold of her arm and walked her to the stairs.

'You first.'

Anne-Marie was incapable of refusing. She climbed three steps before he followed her. She was sure he was staring at her bottom as she moved. She stepped more quickly. When she reached the landing she stopped and glanced back over her shoulder. His gaze stayed low.

'Lead the way,' he said.

She did.

The bedroom door was open. She entered. Their bed was one of the few things they had brought with them. It had not occurred to either her or Marcus to place that in storage. It was a king size model; too big for the room, but they didn't care. 'If you can't have your home,' Anne-Marie had said, 'the next best thing you can have is your bed.'

She stood at the foot of it.

Ethan Hall moved to her right. He placed his left hand on the small of her back. She was wearing Ralph Lauren Grey Marl sweatpants and an Alexander McQueen black T shirt over her underwear. Her feet were bare. She could feel the heat of his palm pressing against her skin.

'Lay on the bed. On the side where you sleep.'

Her mind was empty of all thoughts. She squeezed herself along the left side of the bed. There was a framed photo of her and Marcus on the bedside table, next to a lamp and a book she was reading for the second time. *Tea and Chemo* the story of a woman's battle to overcome cancer. She looked at the bed. She noticed a crease in the pillow. The dark green duvet was smooth and shiny. She laid on it. She could see the sky and the furthest side of the valley through the large bedroom window. Clouds were scurrying across the sky.

'I'm not going to touch you,' Ethan Hall said. 'Not physically.' He closed the door. 'This is going to be the second part of our secret. It's a secret you will want me to keep for the rest of my life. I promise I will. It's a secret I know you will never share.'

Anne-Marie had been drawn to his face from the instant he had started talking; his features filled her vision, she couldn't look away even though he was staring intently at her stomach. She became acutely aware of the waistband of her sweatpants touching her hips, of the material against her thighs, of the rise and fall of her lower abdomen.

'You are scared that you have lost your womanhood,' he said, 'that you are no longer the sexual being you once were. We are both going to enjoy helping you rediscover that.'

'No...'

'Yes.' Ethan clapped his hands together once. 'And the more you try to resist, the more you will be taken by the feelings in ways you never have before. Even as you feel the comfort and support of the bed holding you there, you begin the process of remembering and recreating and moving, from the inside to the out, opening to the inevitability of what is happening, like the currents drawing the tide, making it swell, unstoppable...'

Anne-Marie tried to push herself upright, to swing her feet over the side of the bed. She couldn't move her body. She whipped her head from side to side. Her mouth opened. Her teeth showed. The desire to fight, to escape, was pounding inside in her brain right behind her eyes. She could feel them bulge as she struggled in vain to break free from whatever was holding her.

'That's right! Fight against it!' Ethan's voice was quicker now. He took a step closer to the bed. 'Feel how your heart rate is increasing. Feel how your blood is flowing faster. Feel the tension and how your skin is already tingling. Feel how the inside is already affecting the out. That's it! Your body is preparing you when it spasms like that. It knows how to do this so well. And it has been waiting for you to release it, building secretly, so that here now you can show me. And know this forever, I can see you now. Inside and out.'

And he could. This time he was making a woman orgasm and he wasn't blinded by anger and the need to punish. This time he was far more accomplished. This time watching her was making him hard.

'The paralysis around the internal moving and throbbing and contracting is only there to help you contain it and build it and feel it,' he said, 'knowing it will come out, knowing it will free you. Listen to me now, even with your eyes closed, even as your head thrashes, even when you believe you can't hear me behind the gathering inside you.'

Ethan Hall kept talking. Anne-Marie felt a different part of her brain, in the back of head, urging her to surrender. She forced her head off the pillow and slammed it back several times. The primal desire to give in to her body only increased.

'No!'

She began to feel sweat beading her forehead. Her inner thighs began to tremble.

'No!'

She could feel her blood pulsing and rushing in a way she never had before. She could feel herself swelling and opening. The spasms she had been feeling around her pelvis strengthened and spread.

'No!'

Her breathing quickened. Her mouth was wide open now and she couldn't close it. She was gasping and she couldn't stop it. She couldn't hear his words, but she could feel them. They were on her skin. She could taste them on her tongue. They were entering her.

'Aah!'

It was impossible to stop. She knew it. She hated the part of her that wouldn't be denied. She hated the way her body was betraying her.

'Aah!'

The feelings inside merged, faster than she had ever known before, overwhelming her. The fact that her body couldn't move intensified them further. She began hyperventilating. She knew she was going to explode.

'Say my name when you come,' Ethan said and his words cut through, squeezing her heart.

'No!...No!...'

'Say my name!'

'Aaah!'

'Say it!'

'Ethan!' She screamed as her orgasm sent waves of pleasure crashing through her system. 'Ethan!'

The synesthete saw the power of her experience in ways no one else could. He saw how her body contracted and opened in intimate detail. He saw the colours of her orgasm shooting around her. As her body settled he saw anger and shame robbing her of the satisfaction and comfort she should have been feeling. That excited him even more.

'Good girl,' he said when her breathing had calmed. 'Good girl. Now let's do that again.'

44

Steve the taxi took his newly bought mobile phone out of his jeans pocket for the second time in five minutes. It was a Samsung Galaxy S7. His pride and joy. Well, if push came to shove, he'd have to admit it wasn't as significant as his sixty-five inch, flat screen Panasonic TV. But on the other hand, he couldn't take that out with him. And his phone was more versatile. The marketing – not that he had paid any attention to that – had said the S7 redefined what a phone could do.

And the ability to take photos in the dark was already proving a very particular pleasure.

It was early afternoon now, though. The sky was blue, the clouds white, birds were singing in his back garden. Yet, in a manner of speaking Steve felt that he was in the dark, a different kind of dark to lights out in the bedroom late at night. This was the dark of confusion. The darkness he felt every now and again when one part of him was telling to do one thing, and another part was telling him to do something else.

Steve looked at his phone. He was, he realised, concentrating only on its most basic function. Everything else was temporarily forgotten.

Should he make the call or not?

That was the question. And the important word was should. He could do it. He could do it right now. Or he could wait until later in the day, give himself time to think it all through again, weigh up the pros and cons. He knew for sure that he could do it. He just wasn't sure if he should.

'What a fucker.' Steve scratched the back of his head. He rubbed the palm of his left hand against his jawline, remembered that he hadn't shaved for four days; decided it really didn't matter. This decision mattered. What to do? Spend a couple of minutes making the phone call – for that's all it would take, just two minutes – or to have one last piss and then go out in the taxi. Mull it over as he was driving around. Maybe forget it. Either way, he'd be making some money rather than standing around in his kitchen doing nothing.

Only he was doing something. He was making a decision.

'Or am I just fucking about?'

Steve pursed his lips, exhaled, shook his head. It had been a hell of a lot easier knowing how to vote in the Brexit referendum. Some idiots had wanted to call it a great debate. As far as he was concerned there was no debate needed. In fact, in the weeks leading up to the vote, he had enjoyed telling anyone in the pub who would listen that, when it came to Brexit, he was going to follow the advice his dad had given him about having sex. 'You've got to know when it's time to pull out!' He had said, and when it came to the EU this was it. 'They've been fucking us for long enough,' Steve had proclaimed, laughing each time.

Most people had agreed with him. Job done. Vote won. Easy-peasy.

But what about this fucking phone call?

'Come on, just make your mind up!' Steve walked into the lounge. He looked out of the front window. The big, black Mercedes with the tinted windows was still parked outside the house opposite. In all likelihood, that meant the men he had seen going into the house were still inside. One of the men had looked just like that Ethan Hall character. A proper psycho by all accounts. The man who had been arrested originally for nearly killing Marcus Kline.

Steve had read the interview with Marcus in his morning paper. He wouldn't have bothered normally but he had picked up him once, driven him to the East Midlands airport. He had seemed a surprisingly normal guy. They had chatted about how difficult it was these days making a living as a taxi driver. Marcus had been sympathetic. He'd even offered a couple of suggestions about how to make extra cash. To top it off, he'd tipped him well.

Steve owed Marcus Kline; that's what he couldn't help thinking. And if his dad were still here, he would have told him to make the call. 'We always have to stick together lad,' that's what his dad used to say. 'If we don't have a community we don't have anything. That means we follow the rules and we do what's right for each other. Shoulder to shoulder, that's what makes this country great.'

Steve missed his dad. He wouldn't have known how to use the mobile phone, but he wouldn't have thought twice about getting involved. He wouldn't have worried for a second about possible criminal retaliation. He wouldn't have been motivated only by the reward either. He would have called the police because it was the right thing to do.

Steve would have happily given up his TV and his phone for the chance to share just one more pint with his dad. No amount of thinking was ever going to make that happen, though.

'There's no need to think about this anymore either,' he told himself.

Steve walked back into the kitchen.

Decision made.

Dad was right.

He dialled the number.

45

Peter Jones could feel it all happening around him. Visits, conversations, pressure being exerted. He was the focal point, the required calm at the centre of the storm. Whilst everyday folk went about their everyday business, the criminal world was being shaken, fractures being created or stretched, promises and threats being made and left to work their magic.

Sooner or later something – someone – had to give. That was one of the laws of nature that underpinned the laws of man. If your team is big enough and coordinated and disciplined and it walks in the right directions making the right noises, birds fly. All you have to do then is make sure they don't get away.

Peter wished this were as easy as beating. He wished the stakes were as low. He wished something would come of the undergrowth sooner rather than later.

Beyond his professional responsibilities, he didn't know how much more of this Marcus and Anne-Marie could take. The threat of Ethan Hall was clearly damaging them. He had never seen Marcus so psychologically low, so close to break-down. Once, he would never have thought it possible. Now it seemed as if Marcus was, indeed, hanging on by his fingertips. And, if Anne-Marie was to be believed, she had given up in her fight against her cancer. She was convinced she was going to die and she couldn't tell Marcus. Both husband and wife were, it seemed to Peter, currently imprisoned inside themselves. Locked in solitary confinement with no apparent way out, at least until Ethan Hall was caught. Then, maybe, there was a chance for some sort of return to normality. Maybe.

'Boss!' It was Kevin McNeill, excited, smiling.

'What is it?' Peter controlled his face, kept his body still, calmness at the centre of the storm.

'We've had a call! We think it's a reliable sighting!'

'Why so sure?'

'The caller reported a black Mercedes outside the property. The registration he gave us ties it to Calvin Brent!'

'OK. And?'

'The caller's also saying that he's absolutely certain he saw Ethan Hall and the driver of the car go into the house an hour ago. And he hasn't seen them come out. And the car's still there.'

Peter sat back in his chair, leaning away from his desk, putting both hands behind his head, interlacing his fingers.

'Well, boss?'

'Do we know if it's one of Calvin's safe houses?'

'We've got nothing on that yet.'

'Is the caller known to us?

'No. And he's not on any of our records. He identified himself as Steve the taxi.'

'You are joking?'

'Nope.'

'I wonder what sort of job he does?' Peter smiled.

Kevin chuckled. 'Good job he doesn't clean bogs.'

'Indeed. If he'd identified himself as Steve the shit stirrer, it's fair to say his call would have been treated differently. What's the address?'

'Ipswich Circus, off Sneinton Dale.'

'Right then. I like the feel of this one, Kev! Let's get on with it. You know the drill. I'll make a call and get a firearms team there immediately.'

'Roger that!'

'And Kev, let's keep this to ourselves. Keep the process going everywhere else, keep the pressure on.'

'In case we miss him again?'

'In case Steve the taxi is taking us for a ride.'

46

Anne-Marie had started crying, great raucous sobs that racked her insides the instant she heard Ethan close the front door behind him. For a moment, she had thought it was over and then a sudden fear made her wonder if he was playing another of his awful games, making her believe he had left when in fact he hadn't.

The possibility threatened to pin her in place the way that he had, but at least now she couldn't feel his words and, more than anything else, she had to get off the duvet and away from the bed.

Anne-Marie forced herself to her feet. Her legs were shaking, her clothes damp with sweat. She stood as still as she could, listening for any sound that suggested he was still in the house. She heard nothing beyond her heart thumping in her chest. She was barely aware of the tears coating her face. What if he was waiting for her? What if she went downstairs and he was standing in the hall? What if he was going to make her do it all again?

Anne-Marie looked around the bedroom for anything she could use as a weapon. The best she could see was a small mirror on the dressing table. She picked it up, clutching it tightly in her right hand, intending to use it as a makeshift club. She stepped out onto the landing. The house was silent. She moved to the top of the stairs; wiped her nose with the back of her left hand, wiped tears from her eyes with the tips of her fingers.

'Get out!' She screamed. 'I will kill you!'

The house groaned. She took a step back automatically. Listened. The noise stopped. She told herself that every house made noises.

'I mean it!' Louder this time. Still no reply. She waited for a second then moved forwards again. The stairs creaked under the pressure of her feet. She had never noticed it before. She kept going. Three more steps and she would be in the hallway.

One.

Two.

Three.

Anne-Marie swung to her left, to face the front door, raising the mirror instinctively. Ethan wasn't there. The door was closed. She spun round towards the kitchen and rushed in, giving her fear no time to prevent her. Safe. Only the lounge remaining. The door was half-closed. She slammed it open and charged inside, screaming as she went.

'Yaah!'

Nothing. Just a room that wasn't hers, indifferent to everything that had happened. The mirror dropped from her grasp. At the same time her mobile phone began to ring and vibrate on the coffee table.

Anne-Marie picked it up, praying silently to see a number she recognized. She did. It shocked her, even in her current state. She accepted the call, having no idea what she was going to hear or say.

'Y-Yes?'

'Anne-Marie?'

'Yes.'

'It's me, Emma.'

'I know. I wouldn't delete your number. You're a friend.'

'Of course. Sorry. You just sounded strange and I wasn't sure if that's because you didn't want to talk to me, or if it's because I'm so nervous about making this call I'm projecting my own emotions.'

'Maybe it's just not a great connection. How are you? Why

are you nervous?'

'I'm … er … It's because, er … Well, I feel like I ran away and left you and I always thought of you – I still think of you – as family and you don't run away from your family when things are bad and I did and I'm not able to cope with that.'

'You were grieving for Simon and you did what you needed to, what you believed was best at the time. That's all we can ever do. Marcus understands that. So do I. You have nothing to blame yourself for.'

'But I've seen what's happening. It's all getting so much worse. I don't know how you are possibly dealing with it.'

Anne-Marie stifled a sob. 'We're … erm … we're holding on.'

'How is Marcus? I read the newspaper interview. He seemed so different, so I thought I ought to phone you.'

'He's, you know, doing what Marcus does. He's finding his own way through.'

'And you?'

'I'm still trying my best to focus on my treatment.'

'I pray for you.'

'Thank you.'

'I'm sorry, did you mind me saying that?'

'No. No, I appreciate it. Honestly. So, er, so where are you, what are you doing? Anne-Marie realized she was gripping the top of the armchair Ethan had sat in. She pushed herself away.

'I'm down South,' Emma was saying, 'near my parents. I'm feeling stronger again. The distance has helped. Everyone's been telling me it would. That's why I want to come back. I want to be there with you both. I want to help.'

'No! No, that's really not a good idea!' Anne-Marie didn't care if her voice was too loud. The thought of Emma coming back to Nottingham while Ethan Hall was still free was physically painful. She couldn't take any more pain. Not ever again.

'I just want to show my support, do what I can,' Emma said. 'It's what Simon would have done if…if things had been different.'

'But it's not what he would have wanted you to do. And the situation is so dangerous you really have to keep well out of the way, for our sakes as well as your own. Listen to me, Emma! Marcus would tell you the same if he were here. Stay away until it's over!'

Emma fell silent. Anne-Marie waited. Eventually Emma said, 'If you're sure that's what you want me to do.'

'It is. Right now it's more important to us that you are safe than that we see you again soon. Come back when everything is stable. Then we will be able to make a new beginning.'

'Honestly?'

'Yes.' Anne-Marie was lying in the way a photo never should. She hated herself for doing so. Every part of her felt dirty, corrupted. She knew she was going to burn her clothes.

'Can I call you again?'

'Of course you can. Any time. And I'll tell Marcus you've been in touch. We'll both look forward to seeing you when the time is right.'

'I can't wait.'

'Make sure you do.'

'I promise.'

'Good g–' Anne-Marie stopped herself from completing the phrase she had been going to use. Her spine shivered uncontrollably. 'That's really very good. Thank you.'

'You don't have to thank me. I'll, er, call you again sometime soon.'

'I'll be here. Goodbye, Emma.'

'Bye.'

Anne-Marie ended the call. She threw up onto a carpet that wasn't hers.

47

Detective Chief Inspector Peter Jones met the firearms team at Sneinton police station. It was less than half a mile away from Ipswich Circus, a horseshoe shaped road looping off Sneinton Dale, the major thoroughfare that cut through Sneinton, a part of the inner city.

The firearms team was made up of eight officers, seven men and one woman, led by a Sergeant, David Renson, whom Peter had worked with before. He took Renson into a separate room ahead of the formal briefing.

'I'm coming in with you on this one,' Peter said. 'I want you to know that, and to explain why, before I talk to the rest of the team.'

Renson raised an eyebrow. 'That's very much out of the ordinary, boss.'

'I know. However the guy we are going in to get is very much out of the ordinary. I don't know how much you've seen, read or heard about him, but nothing you think you know will prepare you for the threat he poses.'

'We are all aware of Ethan Hall,' Renson said dryly.

'No. You're really not. You're aware of the stories. You haven't been face to face with the man. There's a world of difference. He's like no one you've ever encountered.'

'And he's never had a raid team bearing down on him before. He's never experienced the speed and aggression we bring to the situation.'

'The problem is, there's a very real risk you won't be fast enough. Actually, the risk is that you can't be fast enough.'

'Before he does what?'

'Look at you. Say something. Make a gesture. I don't know.

It's not what he'll do, it's what the effect will be.'

'Which is?'

'He'll get inside someone's head, hypnotise them, take control of their mind. Once he does that, anything could happen. Christ, this guy could make one of your team fire their weapon on the others. He could cause the sort of chaos that would ruin lives and be impossible to explain later.'

Renson considered briefly. Peter could see him trying to make sense of what he had just heard. He gave the Sergeant time. For a whole host of reasons he didn't want to just pull rank, he wanted the team leader genuinely on board.

'Is it really this fucked up?' Renson asked.

'You know me,' Peter nodded his head. 'I wouldn't be telling you this if there was the slightest doubt.'

'We'd better go brief the team, then.'

'Let's.'

The conversation, whatever it had been about, stopped abruptly as the two men entered the room. Eight pairs of eyes looked quizzically at Peter as he strode to the front. He very deliberately looked at each one in turn. He knew precisely the sort of training they had been through and the risks they took. He remembered Liam Hemsall. He dismissed the memory in the forceful way he sometimes ordered an erring officer out of his presence.

Seven men and one woman, all dressed in black, all carrying Smith and Wesson .38 pistols on their belts along with their Tasers, handcuffs and other equipment, all willing to do whatever was asked of them. Peter knew the weapons and the body armour and helmets too often dehumanized them in the eyes of the public, making it easy to think of them as aggressive, potentially lethal machines of the state. He knew better. He understood the humanity inside the uniform.

Seven men and one woman, each ready to stand up and be counted.

'We believe the house we are entering might be a safe house owned by Calvin Brent, who I'm sure you all heard of.' Peter began. 'The best Intel we've got suggests two men inside. One, a larger, bald guy, is the driver. He probably works for Brent, so he might not be too keen to meet you. Our target is the other man, Ethan Hall. He is five feet nine inches tall, lean with dark hair. He is unusually dangerous, and the important word here is unusually. I know you are all accustomed to front line work, but this guy poses levels of threat you have never faced before. I, for my sins, do have a greater insight into what he's capable of. That's why I'm coming in with you.'

As one the team glanced at Renson. He nodded his support.

'Don't worry,' Peter continued. 'I'll stay at the back and out of your way until the search is complete. The ideal scenario is that we hit them so fast they don't have time to run. Do whatever you have to with the driver, but if – when – you find Ethan I want you to back off immediately. Just seal the room he's in and call me. Under no circumstances engage in any form of interaction with him. I will take over from that point on. Is that clear?'

'Crystal,' Renton said, looking at his team.

'There's a large off-street parking area at the front of the house. It's an ex-council semi. The front door opens straight into the lounge. The kitchen is off that to the back. The stairs are in the lounge, facing the front door. Upstairs there are two bedrooms and a bathroom. The rear garden is flat with a lawn and what looks like a six feet high wooden fence on all sides. There's no shed, or anywhere else where someone could hide. Any questions?'

There were none.

'Good,' Renton said. 'That means, Detective Chief Inspector, we are ready to go.'

'Excellent! Let's make this happen!' Peter led them out of the station. No one spoke.

48

Marcus Kline had been walking for several hours. He had actually been trying not to talk to himself or even think too much, but that really hadn't gone very well. *A step too far*, he had told himself in an attempt to lighten his mood.

At first he had not had a specific destination in mind, content simply to be surrounded by, and pass through, the normality of the city. The mind-fog that had threatened to engulf him previously kept pace. He could feel it working to insert itself into the space around him. He knew that was its deceit. He knew it was actually inside him. *From the Inside to the Out* was the title of an article he had once written. Now he was living it in the worst of ways. He tried to breathe it out as he walked.

Overall the city had paid him no heed; at least, as far as he could tell. He had noticed a couple of people pointing at him, but apart from that everyone seemed too wrapped up in their own world to notice him. Which had been a huge relief.

Admitting how he was really feeling to Peter and Anne-Marie had felt like the start of unburdening himself. The honesty of weakness was not something he was used to. Until recently he would never have associated with it. Now it was all he had. So he kept walking, neither away from pain nor towards pleasure, just moving because that was the basic requirement of life, the building block of evolution.

He couldn't save Anne-Marie if he didn't change. He was sure of that. Even if he had the capability to influence cancer, he was emotionally far too close to her to give of his best. And, try as he might, he had failed to find the distance necessary. *How do you tell your wife,* he wondered, *that I can't help you because I love you too much? How can love be a barrier?*

He knew the answer to that, of course. The good old human brain, that most amazing of all things. The greatest of all survival tools. Yet even it depended on the right input and support, and he had been incapable of providing that. The brain ensured that people felt emotions before they thought rationally. If you couldn't control your emotions, you couldn't operate at your best because your brain was directing resources and energy elsewhere. That was at the very heart of his problem. His brain was too busy dealing with the physical and psychological threat posed by Ethan Hall to give him any chance of healing Anne-Marie.

'She's going to die because of me,' he whispered to himself repeatedly. And every time he did, as the fog swirled around him, he simply slowed his pace and kept walking, breathing strongly in and out until his vision cleared. It was whilst doing this thirty minutes ago he had realized where his walk had to take him. And now he had arrived. Southern Cemetery on Wilford Hill, overlooking the city. The place where Simon was buried.

His grave was marked by a stone bearing the inscription *To a Loving Son, Lost too soon.* A bunch of red roses was propped up against it. Marcus had never been here alone before. It was unbelievably quiet and still, a place where it was all too easy to think too much. He chose to talk instead.

'I guess I'm using you as an outlet, an imaginary therapist. I guess you know that, right? Actually, I don't know why I said that because I know you're not there. I know you are...gone. But in my typically selfish way what I need most right now is an imaginary therapist. Not a real one. They'd answer back. Ask questions. Play clever word games that I'd see through and get annoyed by. And I'd use all of that as a distraction from dealing with myself.

'So, anyway, first of all I just want to say I'm not the man you thought I was. Well, maybe I'm not the man I thought I was. Maybe you and Em always had a different perception of me. I don't know. There are a lot of things I don't know at the moment. And those things I do know, I'm struggling to do anything about.

'I should be at home now, but I need space to find my feet again, to get some semblance of control back, to try and lose some things somewhere. Peter is under enormous pressure and Anne-Marie is…well…she is…anyway…They are both insisting I look after myself. It's the worst time ever and they are still caring about me. That almost makes it worse. Even though it doesn't. It makes me feel even weaker, even though it gives me more reason to get back on an even keel. It's all a bloody great paradox, you see? I wanted to be the best in the world. I got what I wanted – or I thought I had – and that turned out to be the doorway to disaster. And it's a disaster because of what it's done to everybody else. To you.

'Technically, of course, I'm going through the early stages of the bereavement cycle and I'm suffering multiple losses in all sorts of different ways. It's to be expected I'm a mess. It's what any normal human being would experience in a situation like this. Not that any of that helps. Not that it helps at all. I've never thought of myself as a normal human being before. And it's a shit time to confront it. Everything has gone crazy and I find out I'm no different to the rest. Where's Superman when you need him, eh?'

'Is he your son?'

Marcus turned sharply, startled by the intrusion. The questioner was a man he presumed to be in his mid-seventies. He was slightly stooped, wearing an aged grey suit that was at least two sizes too big, with a white shirt, a rose-red tie and a Harris Tweed cap. His shoes were brown and polished.

'No. He was, er, a very dear friend.'

The old man peered at the stone. 'No age at all,' he said. 'That makes it all the worse.'

'Yes.'

'My old lass is over there,' he pointed with a gnarly finger. 'A couple of years now. Most of you goes with them, you know, when it happens. And then the emptiness takes over. It's everywhere. Like it's been waiting for you. Still, I keep telling her it won't be long.' He looked out at the view across the rooftops. 'Mind you, by and large, life keeps going on, doesn't it?'

'Yes it does,' Marcus said, as they shared each other's pain.

49

The firearms team split into two and travelled in separate police vans along Sneinton Dale. Peter sat in the leading van with the officers who would enter through the front door. The journey time was only a couple of minutes. The officers in the second van turned left onto Skipton Circus, a road looping behind Ipswich Circus.

Seconds later, the van Peter was travelling in eased its way into Ipswich Circus and stopped. This was the last delay. They would wait until two members of the first team had successfully made their way to the rear of the neighbours' houses and warned everyone to stay inside with doors locked. With that done, the officers would then position themselves so they were out of any possible line of fire from upstairs windows, but able if necessary to prevent anyone escaping from the back of the house.

Peter hoped they wouldn't be needed. He wanted Ethan Hall contained. He wanted whatever problems they were going to face – and he was secretly sure there were going to be some – to be addressed out of sight of the general public. The last thing he needed was the arrest of Ethan Hall with all its associated challenges filmed from a kitchen window and becoming a YouTube sensation.

The message they were waiting for finally came through via Renton's body mic. He spoke briefly in response. 'They are in position,' he said. 'Let's move!'

The five officers straightened slightly. Peter felt their adrenaline levels rise. He noticed how they all adjusted their posture and breathing to control it. For his part, he kept his body still and his face emotionless. His mind wanted him to visualize Ethan Hall. He silently told his mind to fuck off.

Thirty seconds later the van pulled onto the parking area at the front of the house. The raid team was out in an instant. Peter, Renton and two other officers held back slightly as two of the team went straight for the front door. It was locked. But only briefly.

'Big key!' Renton confirmed to the man holding the specially designed battering ram. The Enforcer, as it was formally known, could hit with more than three tonnes of impact. The door lock was no match. It opened on the first blow.

Renton and his two officers stormed in to the lounge, pistols drawn. Renton was carrying a large, bulletproof shield. He shouted, 'Armed police! Put down your weapons!'

As the door swung to the right, one officer automatically stayed left by the foot of the stairs, the second moved to his right, following the door. Renton took the middle ground. The room was small and square, with a leather ivory coloured three-piece suite and a small coffee table in the centre. There was a pair of coffee cups on the table, but the people who had been using them were not present.

'We're clear!' Renton said.

Peter entered with one of the other officers. The final two remained outside, looking for signs of activity in the front upstairs bedrooms. Everything was happening with the speed and professional assertiveness Peter had expected. The intention was to shock and disorientate the inhabitants, to minimize both the risk of resistance and, in the longer term, any suggestion that the inhabitants had not known who they were.

The man by the stairs stayed in place as Renton led a fast and thorough check of the kitchen. 'Clear!' he announced for the second time. The word had no sooner left his mouth than he was making his way upstairs, the other officers right behind him.

'Armed police! Put down your weapons!'

Peter heard their footsteps on the landing, a door being opened, more shouting and a rush of movement. Then, 'Clear!' Then it all happened again. Only this time the voice changed. This time it had even more authority. This time it was instructing someone.

'Armed police! Put down your weapon! Put down your weapon! Do it now! Do it!'

The officer with Peter stepped forward a pace, peering up the stairs, his gun pointing. Peter forced himself to hold back.

'Stay completely still!' Renton shouted. 'Stay on your knees and don't move! Do not move!' A brief pause and then, 'Boss!'

The officer glanced over his shoulder and nodded, but Peter was already on his way. An officer was standing with his back to him in the doorway of the bedroom at the far end of the landing. His pistol was clearly raised and aimed.

'Jones here!' Peter shouted as he approached. The man didn't look, just made enough space for Peter to step inside. Renton was to the right with his shield and pistol in position. The second officer was on the left of the room, with his back to the wall and his pistol pointed. Ethan Hall was sitting on the edge of a double bed.

A much larger, shaven-headed man wearing a black tee shirt and black Levi jeans was kneeling in front of Ethan, facing the door. He was holding a kitchen knife in both hands, pressing the point down in the space between his trapezius muscle and his collarbone. The sub-clavian artery was only a few centimetres below the skin. It would take virtually no effort and the merest fraction of a second to puncture it. If that happened blood would spurt. It would be potentially impossible to apply pressure to the wound and stop the bleeding. The man would lose consciousness and in all probability die within anything from two to twenty minutes.

Peter kept his gaze fixed on the man with the knife as he assessed the situation. 'Sergeant,' Peter said, 'I want you and your men to sing a song in your heads. Focus on that and nothing else. Sing it loud and big and bold. If you find that becomes difficult even for a second, you need to say. Is that clear?'

'Clear.' Renton's voice was firm.

Peter gestured gently towards the knife. 'Why don't you put that down,' he said quietly, inching forwards as he spoke.

'Stay back!' Ethan said. 'If any of you step over that mark there,' he gestured to a black stain on the laminate flooring, 'my friend here will drive the full length of the blade all the way in, penetrating irreversibly. He'll do the same if I stop breathing. Or if I just tap him on his shoulder, which I am sure I could manage to do even if you did something terrible such as wound me.'

Peter stopped moving. He concentrated hard on the man with the knife. His eyes were glazed, his breathing surprisingly rhythmic. He seemed to have no awareness of what was going on around him. Or the danger he was in.

'He's so calm,' Ethan said, 'because we have had words; words over a brief yet very significant period of time. I'm sure you all know how easy it is to take in the meaning of what is being said, even without meaning to. After all it would be mean not to. And this is meaningful right here and now, I would say. So when I tell you Detective Chief Inspector there really is nothing you can say or do to make him release the knife I am sure that you, just like him, get my meaning.'

Peter resisted the temptation to blink. His mouth was dry. He felt as if he was suddenly struggling with a rapidly forming concussion. 'Nothing we could do, eh?' He forced the words out.

'Not at all. Ethan scratched his nose.

Peter felt his own skin itch.

'Shall I make him push it in a tiny, little bit just to prove my point, so to speak?

'No! No. I believe you.'

'Can't you look me in the face when you say that?'

Peter felt his head nod. His mind, he realised as if from a distance, was already betraying him. He was about to answer the question by saying 'Yes' and looking at Ethan Hall when Renton said, 'Boss, we're waiting for direction!'

The words impacted with the force of a slap to the face. Peter gasped and said, 'Sergeant, you and your men need to stand off. Move out onto the landing now. Keep singing the song as you do so. Move!'

Peter led the way and the team backed out behind him. 'Are you all OK?' He asked.

The men nodded, but their eyes showed a degree of confusion. He guessed that his probably did, too. He nodded his thanks to Renton.

'You armour is bulletproof, not word-proof,' Peter said. 'Ethan wants to make us look at him and listen to him. If he hypnotizes even one of us this is all going to hell. We have to watch out for each other in ways we never have. We have to keep checking that we're all OK, that we're keeping him out. Does everybody understand?'

The team nodded.

'Your communal fear and confusion is lighting up the landing,' Ethan said loudly. 'The least you could do is close the door.'

'What's your so-called friend's name?' Peter asked.

'It really doesn't matter. You can call him Lazarus, if you like.'

'We know he works for Calvin Brent, which means you've

got yourself into the big league. Not that it matters anymore. You see, any professional criminal would tell you that once it gets to this stage there's only one conclusion. So, as we are sharing truths, you need to know the only place you're going from here is jail. All you are doing by threatening that man and delaying us is adding years to your sentence.'

'You are presuming too much. If you knew me better, you'd know that I really only help people to find their own way. I'm acting like this because I'm terrified of what you might do to me. You threatened me in hospital. That's why I had to leave, even though I was – I still am – in such poor health. I'm the one being persecuted here. I'm the one acting out of character.'

Renton shook his head in disbelief.

'I'm not going to talk to you anymore, Ethan.' Peter said. 'I'm calling in professional negotiators. Two of them, so they can guard each other against you.'

Ethan laughed. 'You don't seriously think you have anyone who can get inside my head, do you?'

'Who knows? Besides, it seems to me the only way to end this thing is for one of us to gamble. And that's going to be me.'

'Really? What are you going to do?'

'That would be telling. But remember, the man you're holding hostage is a villain. We'll have all the info we need about him any time soon. I'm guessing he's a really bad boy. Which means he's not as valuable to you as a normal member of the public would be. You get what I mean?'

Ethan hesitated only briefly. 'You wouldn't risk this man's life.'

Peter grinned. Want to bet?' He said.

50

'Willingly,' Ethan replied, 'because if you really are planning to gamble the meaning is clear. You recognize that I have all the power here and there's nothing you can logically do. So, listen, why don't you take a deep breath, come back in and we can talk?'

'I'll stay where I am, thanks.'

'Peter, I can't believe you don't really want to do this yourself. Where is the hunter inside you? Do you really want to stand back and let the negotiators try? Thinking about it now. Deeply. Aren't you going to step in the right direction, finding out what is happening here? Isn't that your job? Peter? Isn't that what being an Inspector means?

Renton saw the DCI frown, lick his lips, glance at the bedroom. He reached out and squeezed Peter's shoulder hard, demanding his attention. 'Stay with us, boss!' He whispered forcefully.

'Yes! Thanks!' Peter brought his focus back to bear.

Renton took out his notebook and wrote, *What's the plan?*

'Ethan you clearly don't know me as well as you think you do,' Peter spoke loudly, giving deliberate emphasis to every word. 'I'm interested only in the process and the result. This isn't about me. It's never about me. That's the difference between us – that and the fact I'm part of the best team in the world and you're on your own.'

Peter took Renton's notebook and pen. He wanted to write but nothing came to mind. He stared blankly at Renton's words. It was a very good question. In fact, it was the only question right now. What the hell was the plan?

'Aah, but I'm not on my own, am I? My friend is listening

and every time I speak his state deepens, and who know what will happen because you refuse to play and we hear with our ears even the cutting words of others,' Ethan's voice softened, becoming lyrical in tone, 'and words are just vibrations, so sharp they burst with meaning and sometimes pain and sometimes thinking about the feeling drums up an urgency because we are all unconscious beings first and…'

'Sing to yourselves!' Peter ordered. 'Activate your minds and keep your eyes fixed on each other! The team wins!'

'…When suddenly you realise the answer is at hand,' Ethan continued, 'because there is so much noise, bursting out and bursting in and even here there is one way to escape if you just cut through the distractions so easily and then return as if nothing has happened because what you cannot feel you cannot need to…sink even deeper…now…all the way…down.'

The voice stopped. Peter checked the three men around him. Thumbs up from each one. He breathed a sigh of relief. Then fragments of what Ethan had been saying came back to him and his stomach froze.

'Ethan, what's happening in there?'

'We're just waiting for you to come in and play.'

Renton grabbed Peter's upper arm. He shook his head.

'So nothing has changed?' Peter asked.

'Everything changes. You know that.'

Peter broke free of Renton's grip, let the notebook drop, and took one pace into the room. Ethan grinned. 'Welcome.'

The left side of the big man's face was covered in blood. His left ear was on the floor at his side. The knife was back in place above his sub-clavian artery. He appeared to be breathing normally.

'Jesus!'

'It used to be called cropping,' Ethan said. 'An act of physical punishment dating back to ancient times and cultures. The Babylonians were into it. The Assyrians, too. We, of course, were late to the party, but by the time of Henry the eighth vagrants would have their ears cut off for a second offence. It's one of the potential hazards of sitting around having nowhere to go, I guess.'

'You're a sick bastard!'

'I didn't do it,' Ethan raised both hands. 'Look, there's not a drop on me. No, he did it to himself. Unprovoked. Well, I say unprovoked, I'm sure it was a consequence of your threatening and abusive behaviour.'

Sergeant!' Peter called.

'Boss?'

'Check how long before the negotiators get here. And the sniper, too!'

'Ooo,' Ethan cocked his head. 'You didn't mention a sniper.'

'I told you I was going to gamble.'

'Shoot me and he dies,' Ethan reminded. 'You won't be able to get to him quickly enough.'

'My Sergeant is faster than he looks.'

'I doubt that.' Ethan glanced out of the window. 'Talking of shooters, whatever happened to your man who shot me? I imagine he's been struggling terribly. I really hope you haven't hung him out to dry.'

'Bastard!' Peter turned to go and then looked back. 'Whatever the deal you've struck with Calvin Brent, I reckon when he hears about this,' he pointed at the severed ear, 'and I promise you he will hear all the details, he's going to be very unhappy with you. I reckon I might be the least of your worries.' Peter walked out.

'How are you feeling?' Renton whispered.

'Fucking angry.'

'But not, you know,' Renton tapped his own temple, 'spaced out or anything?'

'No. That wasn't his aim this time.'

Renton had retrieved his notebook. He wrote, *Do you actually want negotiators and a sniper?*

Peter shook his head.

Renton wrote, *Then what?*

'You've gone very quiet out there,' Ethan said. 'You're not trying to hide from me, are you? That wouldn't help anyone now would it? To be honest with you, I can't help but wonder how much longer it will be before the stress makes my friend hurt himself again. I'm sure you know the only way to avoid that is to let us both leave here free as birds. The longer it goes on like this, the worse it gets for all of you.'

Renton wrote, *Boss?*

Peter realized he was smiling. The phrase was fresh in his mind, crisp as the best October morning. *Free as birds.* That was it! He had forgotten how best to flush out Ethan Hall. Noise and movement. Still a gamble, but less so than anything else.

Peter took Renton's notebook and printed his instructions in capital letters. He showed them to each member of the team. Thumbs up. No questions.

'No one out here is trying to hide from you, Ethan. And just to prove the point...' He stepped back into the bedroom, moving to the right of the open door.

'Well, look at you!' Ethan applauded briefly. 'You've come back into the arena.'

'I thought we were the ones persecuting you.'

'Most people in the gladiatorial arena were innocents, captured and forced to defend themselves. You really should spend more time reading Peter; broaden your knowledge. You are going to have more time at home to read, aren't you -'

Peter flinched.

' – when our business together is finished?'

'I want to tell you how this is going to play out,' Peter said.

'Wouldn't you rather, looking at me now, just stop all that internal fighting because that is the real arena, you know, the place where meanings are born, where they grow almost – '

'Remember the fields, boss!' Renton shouted. Peter's body jolted back under control, like a man resisting sleep. 'Remember the fields!'

Peter looked at his watch. Then he spoke quickly. 'I want you to know the sniper will be here inside five minutes. You previously attacked a police officer with a lethal weapon. You pose a lethal threat. You are holding a hostage. Your life is very much at risk.'

'I didn't attack your officer; I was trying to surrender. You're just misinterpreting what you saw. Surface structure. Nothing more Peter. And it's not what happens on the surface that creates meaning, it's what is happening deep, deep inside, all the way down, as you –'

'The fields!' Renton shouted. 'Keep walking through the fields!'

Peter regained control. It was harder this time. He imagined he was moving forward, disturbing the cover, flushing out his prey. His voice was loud and fast. 'My officers are under orders to stay out of the room, but you need to think about the sniper and the negotiators and Calvin Brent and the fact that sooner or later bullets always silence words. You're out of your depth, you've got lots to think about and process and such little time to do it.'

'You are so wrong!' Ethan Hall was louder too. His face was red with anger. 'I am in control! I –'

'– You are nothing more than a bird on the run!' Peter shouted. 'Too stupid to know when your time has come! There is too much, too much, too much, going on and there's only you squawking and fluttering like it means anything – '

' – I am hunting you!' Ethan screamed as Renton charged into the room, staying short of the black mark, a Taser in his hands instead of his pistol. At the same time, the three officers on the landing shouted, 'Sniper at the window! Sniper! Look out!'

Ethan was already reaching for Matt's shoulder, but he couldn't prevent himself from taking one quick glance at the window. It was all the time Renton needed. He Tasered Matt in the chest, the wires crackling out, hitting him flush in the right pectoral. The big man groaned. His body trembled and he collapsed forwards, dropping the knife. Ethan leapt off the bed, stretching for the weapon. Peter hit him side-on, wrapping his arms around Ethan's upper body, taking them both to the floor. He felt an unexpected surge of energy as the synesthete fought to shake himself free. For a second he feared he wouldn't be able to hold him, then help arrived. Hard and fast. Peter staggered upright as Ethan was pinned to the floor and handcuffed.

'Call for an ambulance,' Peter said to Renton.

'On it.'

Ethan was pulled to his feet. 'Get this piece of shit out of here,' Peter ordered. 'Let's get him in a cell where he belongs. And keep talking to each other all of the time.'

He took a moment to watch the officers march Ethan along the landing. He listened to their footsteps on the stairs, to the front door opening, to a van door closing.

'Good job, boss.' Renton said.

'Couldn't have done it without you.'

'Beating for birds, eh? That was at the heart of the master plan.'

Peter shrugged, allowed himself a half-smile. 'Pheasants are easier,' he said.

51

In the end, when the necessary paperwork had been done, he texted the news to Marcus and Anne-Marie. It affected them both differently. To Marcus it seemed anti-climatic. To Anne-Marie, distant and insignificant. She thought she ought to feel triumphant, avenged, but could summon no emotion. They tried to talk about it that night, in the lounge with the stained carpet. Marcus sat in the same armchair Ethan Hall had.

'I know change can happen in an instant,' Marcus said, 'but this feels somehow unreal, otherworldly. If you told me we live in a world of ghosts and I'd just never realized it before, well...' His voice trailed off.

'Perhaps we do live in a world of ghosts. And if we do, perhaps they see us as the otherworldly beings.'

'Don't do that to me. I'm struggling to make sense of everything as it is. It's as if Ethan has been right in front of me, in my face night and day, whether I've been awake or asleep, and now suddenly he's not there and it feels like something is missing.'

'Something is.'

'Yes, but it feels like something else is missing as well as Ethan.' He considered for a moment. 'What do you think the difference is between space and emptiness?'

'I, er, I think emptiness is one of the myriad things we can create in space.'

Marcus sat back. 'Wow! Where did that come from?'

'I've been doing a lot of thinking and reflecting lately.'

'Of course. Sorry.'

'Don't be silly. I love you.'

'I love you, too. I have no emptiness where you – we – are concerned.'

'I know.'

'I'm surprised Peter didn't come round in person to deliver the news,' he said, changing the subject because love was also a barrier.

'I guess he's still got a lot on. And it's been incredibly hard for him too. I wouldn't be surprised if he just wanted to get home to Nic.'

'Yeah. I'm sure you're right. I can't blame him for wanting to be with his partner rather than having to manage me. I think I owe him a case of exceptionally good red wine.'

'I doubt he feels you owe him anything.'

'All the more reason to show my thanks – and reinforce my apology.'

'It's a nice idea. I'm sure, though, that your relationship is back to where it was before all of this.'

'I hope so.' Marcus looked at the carpet. 'Let's do a hypnosis session first thing in the morning.'

'That will be great.'

'I think so, too.'

'And maybe we should start looking.'

'For?'

'Our next proper home.'

'Are you serious?'

'One hundred percent.'

'Let's do it then.' Anne-Marie hid everything else behind her smile. She felt different inside. She had ever since she had thrown up. The trance states Ethan Hall had put her in were the most powerful she had ever known. If, in some incredible way, he had started her healing process it would be the cruelest form of punishment she could imagine. What he did to her afterwards made everything indescribably worse. Now she doubted and distrusted herself in ways she never had. And she could no longer remember what Marcus's touch felt like.

'Great! I'll get the local papers and have a look online tomorrow.' He said.

'That's going to be very exciting!'

Anne-Marie knew she would take the secret of Ethan Hall's visit to her grave.

52

One week later Peter Jones met with Mike Coopland, his friend and the barrister he had ensured would be prosecuting the Ethan Hall case. They met every week in Mike's local Indian restaurant. Their routine was always the same. Peter drank only a pint of lager because he was driving, and ate a king prawn balti. Mike drank more because he was within walking distance of his home and ate whatever took his fancy on that particular night.

Mike was a huge man, a former bodybuilder, with a love of modern jazz that bordered on obsession.

This was their first meeting since Ethan's arrest. And since Peter had informed his friends of Nic's departure.

'How are you coping?' Mike asked.

'As well as anyone could be,' Peter said.

'To be fair you ought to, you've got more experience than most.'

'Some pains hurt more than others.'

'Fair point.' Mike emptied nearly half of his pint glass in one swallow. 'So the summary is, you're unlucky in love but lucky at work. After all, it couldn't have worked out much better with Ethan Hall.'

'He could have stayed in his hospital bed.'

'True. But once he upped sticks he could have caused a lot more harm than he did. Essentially you're telling me that he got out, got involved with Calvin Brent, and got himself arrested before he could do any damage.'

'Any damage that we know about.'

'If no one hears the tree fall in the forest, does it make a noise?'

'Fuck off.'

'I'm just saying. If he did something and we never get to know about it, it's not our concern.'

'It doesn't mean it didn't hurt people.'

'Some pains are quieter than others.'

'Fuck off again.'

Mike finished his beer and ordered another. 'This guy has got under your skin, hasn't he?'

'More than anyone. It's not because of his crimes, it's because getting under your skin is what he's best at. He gets into your mind and influences you. Even when you don't want to be influenced. Even when you're fighting with everything you've got to stop him. I thought Marcus was way out on his own in the way he can get inside your head and lead you to places you didn't think possible. I was wrong. Ethan is in a different league.

'I'm telling you, Mike, even when we had him penned in a corner it was like he was ready for us. He behaved as if he was in control all the way through – until we managed to throw him off just long enough for us to jump him. Even then it was touch and go.

'This is the first time I'm asking you to prosecute someone and I can't tell you I know the extent of their power. He does things with words and looks and gestures that make guns seem limited.'

'A courtroom is a different place. It has its own culture and rules. You know that. Ethan doesn't. His trial is going to be a whole new experience for him. He is going to be in my world, not his.'

'But you are going to have to put him on the stand.'

'And if I do, he's going to be dancing to my beat.'

'You're not getting it,' Peter leant across the table. 'I had to pull all of the firearms officers out of the room. He was hypnotizing them. And me. If I hadn't been expecting him to do such a thing none of us would have escaped. And being ready for him only bought me an extra few seconds. I'd have been toast if it hadn't been for Renton talking to me when he did.'

'Have you considered the possibility that, because you knew all the stories about him, you were preconditioned to be susceptible to a force that might not have been there?'

'This is me you are talking to.'

'And by your own admission, you regard Ethan as a most special human being. It's absolutely possible you are over-egging this guy. After all, and I don't mean this in anyway to be an indictment of your own ability because I know just how very good you are, Ethan's locked up right now. For the second time. If he is such a superstar, how come you've caught him twice in such a short space of time?'

'Because he doesn't know the rules of our game.'

'Exactly! The prosecution rests.' Mike turned his attention to his beef madras.

Peter sipped his beer. Over the last week he had been thinking a great deal about Ethan Hall. The synesthete was now in prison awaiting trial. At Peter's urging, he had been isolated from the general population and was under constant supervision in a single cell in the hospital wing.

There was a good reason why Ethan Hall was a loner and why Darren Smith had wanted him out of his house. The notion of actually living with Ethan was absurd and frightening.

Who'd have thought I'd have something in common with that sick fuck?

The thought stabbed like a knife. Peter let it go, reminding himself not for the first time that there was enough pain in the world without creating your own personal batch.

No, it wasn't Ethan's brief time with Darren Smith that was scratching at his insides; it was the Calvin Brent connection. There was no way the gangster would have helped Ethan without demanding something in return. And he would have expected payment in advance. So what had Ethan done for him? The answer to that question held the key to unlocking the whole thing. Only no one was offering an answer. Brent certainly hadn't when Peter visited him five days ago. The Numbers Man had played his poker face, insisting he had never met Ethan, that Matt had been acting of his own accord and had then become the innocent victim of a cornered madman. Beyond that there had been no reports of any crimes suggesting Ethan's involvement.

Silence reigned.

Only that didn't make everything all right. In fact, potentially it made things worse. Mike was wrong. If a tree fell in the forest and no one heard it, there was still a tree down. If enough trees fell unseen and unheard the result would still be the same: nature herself would be changed and the consequences would be catastrophic.

Peter Jones looked at his curry and realized he had lost his appetite. His gut was telling him something was wrong. He just didn't know what.

53

You know it isn't over, don't you?

A part of you is desperate to believe it is, but that part of you is made up of weakness, desperation and denial.

It always ends after it ends.

I thought you knew that by now. I thought you might have learnt something. I thought you might have realised that I have been in control every step of the way. Everything you have done. Every thought. Every action. Every emotion. Every decision. All determined by me.

Do you really think I need to be in the room to influence you? Do you really think bricks and mortar or time and space restrict me? Do you really think influence is so easily contained?

If that were the case, the past could never limit or move you. The future couldn't inspire or scare you. The words you heard yesterday would not replay, unbidden, in your mind and affect the way you feel. And yet they do, don't they?

If that were the case, you would be able to grow or dissolve your beliefs with ease. Only you can't, can you?

You have no idea how to manage your beliefs because the influence that created them follows their scent no matter where you run, it tracks them down and finds its way in no matter how firmly you lock the door.

You cannot escape me because I know how to tighten the beliefs that bind. Just as I know how to release them and replace them with something even worse.

This is the great truth of it all. You are still the herd, rushing towards the edge, thinking you have made the best of decisions yet staring up at the ceiling in the middle of the night fearful and wondering. I look up in the middle of the night and see the future. Yours. The one I am about to create.

So please do just one more thing for me: enjoy this time if you can.

Do everything in your power to make this brief spell feel safe and good and true. Cling for all you are worth because I haven't finished with you yet. I'm not even close to finishing with you.

There is a war coming.

Believe me.

Marcus Kline – and Ethan Hall – will return in

Faith, Summer 2018.

ACKNOWLEDGEMENTS

Marcus Kline, the world's greatest communication guru, owes his existence to four people: Mairi, Alan, Matthew and IbA.

Mairi helped bring him to life during two fabulous weeks in France.

Alan provided great knowledge about campaigning communications and was instrumental in the selection of Marcus's hair styling.

Matthew ensured that this, the second part of Marcus's story, is now in your hands.

IbA started it in the mid-1970s when he began teaching me how to read the lines on peoples' faces.

I am – and will always be – grateful to you all.

DCI Peter Jones, the great detective and Marcus Kline's best friend, owes all of his wisdom and professional ability to PJ. Big thanks to him for the adoption and the insights.

Chris Parker is a specialist in Communication and Influence.
His fascination with the power of words and how they can be
used to create intrapersonal and interpersonal change began
in 1976. It became a lifelong study that has underpinned
almost four decades of work in a variety of professional
roles and contexts. A Licensed Master Practitioner of Neuro
Linguistic Programming (NLP), Chris is a highly-experienced
management trainer, business consultant, lecturer and writer.
He has more lines on his face than most and is afraid to read
them.

Chris is also the author of thriller *Influence* (the first in
the Marcus Kline trilogy) and two critically acclaimed poetry
volumes, *Debris* and *The City Fox*.

"I was reading Chris Parker 20 years ago. He was amazing
then and he is amazing now."
– Geoff Thompson, BAFTA winning screenwriter

INFLUENCE – paperback
£6.99
ISBN 9781909273061

Influence kills...Influence is the greatest force on earth. Influence equals power, the power to affect people and events. The most powerful people alive have the greatest influence. And they can use it for good or bad. Marcus Kline is the world's leading authority on communication and influence. He can tell what you are thinking. He can see inside you. He can step inside your mind. Yet when a series of murder victims bear the horrific hallmarks of an intelligent and remorseless serial killer, Detective Inspector Peter Jones turns to Marcus for help – and everything changes.

As the killer sets a deadly pace, the invisible, irresistible and terrifying power of influence threatens friendships, reputations, and lives. When events appear to implicate the great Marcus Kline himself, everyone learns that the worst pain isn't physical...

URBANE

Urbane Publications is dedicated to
developing new author voices, and publishing
fiction and non-fiction that challenges, thrills and
fascinates.

From page-turning novels to innovative
reference books, our goal is to publish what
YOU want to read.

Find out more at
urbanepublications.com